A Crack in the Glass

Charles Owen

Telling Tales: Vol 1

Books by Charles Owen

Novellas:

FIAMMA

CRY CASSANDRA !

Telling Tales:

Vol 1: A CRACK IN THE GLASS

Vol 2: THE MARK OF THE BEAST

Vol 3: MAN OVERBOARD

Vol 4: ESCAPADE

Copyright

Published by Charles B. Owen.

Copyright © Charles Owen 2015

Cover photograph by: Tanis Saucier / www.shutterstock.com
Cover design by: Sarah Pearson.

This book is a work of fiction. All characters and events in this book are fictitious, and any resemblance to actual persons living or dead, businesses, companies, events, or locales is purely coincidental.

Paperback ISBN: 978-0-9930399-7-3
Ebook mobi ISBN: 978-0-9930399-6-6

CONTENTS

The Glass Pane

Major Donald Tremlett slammed the garage door behind him. He limped into the sitting room, picked up the telephone and dialled a number.

'Lister Inquiry Agents. Ron Lister speaking.'

Tremlett winced at the sound of the man's rough vowels. His wife was on the train, he said. She would be at Victoria Station at six o'clock.

'If the train is not delayed. You realise that it will be priced as an evening job.'

'I have your price list.' Money – that's all those parasites were interested in. 'You have the photograph of her?'

He had it. 'What is Mrs Tremlett wearing?'

'A grey coat and skirt … a headscarf … and she may be carrying a mackintosh.'

'I will see to it myself.' Who else. Lister's eyes flickered around the empty office with its peeling wallpaper and rows of grubby files.

'I don't want her approached.' Tremlett raised his voice. 'All I want to know is–'

'Where she goes and who she sees.' The old buzzard was beginning to get on his nerves.

'Correct. And report back.' He mopped his forehead. He did not mean it to sound like a parade-ground bark but it had been a trying morning.

He threw off his coat and tie. Whatever had happened to respect for your elders and betters? Another casualty of the war, he supposed. War seemed to have been with him all his life. First The Great War. Then an interval in which people seemed to do nothing except ask themselves when the next one was coming. Then it had.

He was adjutant of a training battalion in Surrey in that first show. He tried to get to the Front but they wouldn't let him go. You are bloody good at your job, Tremlett. Too valuable to lose. Anyone can go to France and be blown to bits. But only one in a thousand can turn a yokel into a first-rate soldier inside a few months. So he stayed. Finished the war as a major.

He was too old this time around. A few nights a week on fire-watching was all he could cope with. Julia's death and then Peggy's was a hard knock. First his daughter, then his wife. Men can fall apart for less reason and for a time he did lose his bearings.

When Lucy came into his life he was at a low ebb and in a moment of weakness he agreed to marry her. She was a pretty creature with her fair hair and her WAAF uniform which showed off her trim figure. She did a job that he admired, she was a tolerably good cook and a pleasant companion. Above all, her life seemed to be organised and disciplined and, so far as he could judge, free of entanglements.

The chaps at his club probably wondered what the hell the girl saw in him and he came in for some good-natured ribbing. Overweight he might be, and losing his hair, but he could offer her security, a rock to cling to in these turbulent times and that was beyond price.

Lucy was working too hard. A week's leave would put her right if she slowed up a bit. He was uneasy at the thought that they would be thrown together so much for they hardly knew each other. Then those trips to London, often returning on the last train. He didn't like to interrogate her but who the devil was she seeing?

That man in the photograph? The heavy cardboard envelope had arrived by special messenger! If that was not brazen, what was! It had taken him half an hour to open it and reseal it without leaving any traces.

A young man in RAF uniform stared out at him. A flight lieutenant. In a corner it simply said, 'Love from Johnny'. An officer and a gentleman does not open another fellow's mail but neither does he sit back and allow himself to be made a fool of. Something has to give. He reached for his old briar pipe and sucked gloomily on the stem. If there was one thing that he hated, it was disloyalty – and indiscipline ran it a close second. Lucy must pack in this nonsense … or else. He did not want to think about the else.

***

Lucy Tremlett settled back into her seat with a sigh and closed her eyes. A whistle, a snort of steam and the train pulled away from the platform. Her tired mind was like a chaotic sewing basket, a jumble of multicoloured threads, short ends all of them.

The Senior Air Staff Officer had been adamant. Lucy, what you need is a complete break. The Ops Room is no place for people who are exhausted. Admit it. You are at the end of your rope. If you cannot shake off yesterday's bad news you are no use to the men in the air today. So, off you go! Get the Major to take you away for a few days. And, by the way, I am sorry about Johnny. He was a good man.

How different things might have been if she had met Johnny earlier. During the Blitz, she had once spent the day at the Air Ministry in Whitehall. Johnny

Colgrave was working there on secondment from a bomber squadron based near Oxford.

That night there was a heavy raid and it was impossible for her to get home. It was late and they left the building together as soon as the all-clear sounded. His mother, he told her, was dead. Cancer. His father was a naval officer. His destroyer had been sunk in the Norway Campaign and he had been taken prisoner. The family had a flat near Baker Street and he had the use of it. The two of them shared a makeshift supper and afterwards she made a few half-hearted telephone calls in search of a bed for the night but there was not a room to be had.

They talked into the small hours. Lucy learned that he had flown on twelve missions before being rested. Some tiresome scruple led her into telling him about Donald.

She had met her husband a few months earlier in a London underground station during one of the heaviest raids of the war. Outside, buildings, gutted by fire, were toppling into the street. The sky was criss-crossed with white beams searching for the bombers. Down in the docks, even the water was burning.

Donald's house had received a direct hit the week before. His wife was killed instantly. His daughter, their only child, for whom they had spent years waiting, had been lost a few months earlier when the ship on which she was being evacuated to Canada was torpedoed. As she talked to Johnny, one of the images of that night in the shelter came back to her. Donald, caught up in that press of bewildered humanity, leaning on a stick, looking from one face to another like a lost dog. *'Oh,*

God!' she remembered praying at the height of the raid, 'out of this terrible night let some good come.'

She had married Donald and vowed to be a good wife to him. He was almost twice her age. There was so much destruction, so many people were dying, it seemed like a very small sacrifice at the time.

There was a piano in the flat and Johnny played for her, finishing with one of those magical Chopin nocturnes. The magic worked and beyond the blacked-out windows all was hushed. For a few precious minutes the noisy world seemed to have laid aside its quarrels to listen.

Afterwards, she and Johnny sat in silence until the gas fire sputtered and went out. He found her some pyjamas and lent her his bed. He was suddenly so shy and correct that she felt like throwing something at him. Of course he slept on the sofa.

The next day, she heard that Johnny had asked to be transferred back to his squadron. Was it something that she had said? Was it vanity or guilt that made her want to call him. But she thought better of it. After all, what business was it of hers? It had been a very pleasant evening. That was all. One of hundreds of little adventures that happen in wartime. She was married to Donald. She must put Johnny Colgrave out of her head.

But it was not so easy. She and Donald rented a small house in Croydon not far from the airfield where she worked. At night, just as she was getting to sleep, she would hear the drone of the bombers as they set out on another mission. Was Johnny back with his squadron? Was he up there somewhere in the darkness?

Then, one evening, she got home to find an envelope addressed to her. Inside there was a photograph of Johnny. She was cross with him but not as cross as she should have been.

An hour later he called her. 'Hello Lucy. Can you talk?'

'Donald has gone out for a drink, if that is what you mean. Look, Johnny. I don't think the photograph was a very good idea and that goes for this call too.'

'I know. I'm sorry but I am flying again tonight.'

'Where are you calling from?' The idiot. He could be court-martialled for this.

'Don't worry. I'm in a telephone box in the village.' She could hear him putting another coin in the box. 'Mission number thirteen coming up.'

'You don't believe in that superstitious nonsense?'

'Anyone who says that they don't think about it is a liar.'

'You will be alright.'

'Is that a promise?'

'Oh, Johnny. This isn't fair. I can't be your girl.'

'Then, be my good-luck charm.'

'To put in your pocket or hang around your neck like a rabbit's foot?'

'I wouldn't say no!'

Change tack. 'Who is flying with you?'

'I have got my old crew back – Bill Lakin, Mike Maguire, Chalky White and the others.'

'That's wonderful. And their skipper is not going to let them down.'

'Not if I can help it. It's just that I have this presentiment–'

'Johnny – this is morbid. Have a stiff glass of brandy. As soon as you are in the air you will feel quite different.'

He laughed. 'Perhaps you are right. But if I find myself the other side of the glass pane, I will try to–' He was cut off.

That night, she woke up shivering with cold and aching all over. Her nightdress was soaking wet. She was in the garden. Curled up next to the sundial. It was still dark. She must have walked in her sleep. She had not done that since she was a child.

She crept back inside the house and up the stairs. In her bedroom, she changed quickly and got into bed. She could feel the photograph under her pillow. She would send it back to him first thing in the morning.

That night's losses were marked up on the board in the Ops Room. Johnny's Lancaster never got to Essen. Over the Dutch coast it ran into heavy anti-aircraft fire and came down somewhere in Holland. The whole crew was posted missing, believed killed.

***

It was dusk by the time the train drew into Victoria. The pavements were damp and a fine mist hung in the air. Lucy shivered into her mackintosh. The house that she was looking for was in a dark, unlit street close to Vauxhall Bridge but her feet seemed to lead her there as if she had known it all her life.

Once she thought she heard footsteps behind her, but when she stopped to listen, they stopped too. She took a deep breath and knocked on the door. From the other side came a shuffling noise accompanied by what sounded like a whispered argument and when the door was opened, she was surprised to see only the tall, gaunt figure of an elderly lady.

'Good evening, Mrs–'

'Just call me Zelda. Everyone does.'

She followed the stooped figure to a small sitting room. By the dim yellow light of a lantern she could see the remains of a coal fire smouldering in the grate. The woman helped her out of her mackintosh and laid it over an armchair, over which tartan rugs had been thrown.

She gestured towards a hard upright chair drawn up to the table and took one herself. Her hair was white and fell to her shoulders.

As Lucy sat down, a fluttering movement in a corner of the room startled her.

'*Captain!* Mind your manners! That's the parrot. Pay no heed to him.' Zelda placed a hand against the side of a teapot. 'Tea? Or would you like something stronger?'

'Tea will do fine.'

'I always have a pink gin at about this time. My husband was a navy man.' Zelda inclined her head towards a photograph on the mantelpiece and sipped at her glass.

'*Happy landings*!' squawked the parrot from out of the darkness.

Zelda was wearing a long-sleeved black velvet dress with a white fur collar and she teased a handkerchief from under the cuff to wipe the corner of her mouth. Somewhere a clock chimed.

'You came about Flight Lieutenant Colgrave,' said Zelda softly.

'I … I don't remember that I gave a name.'

'But that is the officer you came about,' Zelda repeated. Her long, bony fingers tapped lightly on the table.

'We weren't married … or engaged … or in love … you see, I'm married already ... I hardly knew him…' The words tumbled out before Lucy could stop them. Momentarily overwhelmed, she pressed her lips together and bowed her head in silence.

Zelda stretched across the table and took Lucy's hands in hers. 'My dear, this will do no good.'

Lucy reclaimed her hands. 'Do you mean that there is no hope? His plane disappeared over Holland but nobody saw it go down.'

'I know that you have been asking after him.'

Her eyes widened in surprise but she did not frame the question. 'These past days I have done nothing else. Nobody can tell me anything. I saw your card in the window of a newsagents, so … in desperation…'

'You came to see old Zelda. You would not have done that, my dear, unless in your heart of hearts, you believed that he would not come back.'

Lucy dabbed at her eyes. 'I know. It must seem ridiculous but somehow I still feel responsible for him. His mother is dead and his father is in a prisoner of war camp.'

Her companion gave a deep sigh. 'What is it that you want from me?'

'I don't know. If only I felt that he was at peace.'

'That takes time. You must be patient.'

'How long must I wait?'

'My dear young woman, I cannot tell you. There is so much fear, so much pain, so much anger – it all has to be worked through.'

'And then?'

'Then he may declare himself. Until then, you must leave him alone. I say this for your own good. It could be dangerous.'

Lucy smiled. 'Surely that is rather fanciful. John was the one who ran the risks.'

Zelda pushed back her chair and rose to her feet. 'I am asking you to drop these investigations. Come back and see me in a month. Do this for my sake.'

Lucy dropped her eyes. 'I cannot promise that. Not just yet.' She had been given the name of a club. The Fallen Angel. It was in Chelsea and had the reputation of playing host to rather a fast crowd. It was strictly against orders for servicemen and women to visit it but some of Johnny's squadron had been seen there.

Lucy reached into her handbag but Zelda refused any payment. '*Off Limits! Off Limits!*' the parrot squawked as they made their way to the front door.

Lucy took Zelda's hand. 'I'm sorry,' she said. 'I feel that I have disappointed you.'

Zelda pressed her hand. 'There is no disappointment, my dear, but you look tired and unwell. I confess that I am anxious for you.' The door closed softly.

***

The mist had been replaced by a yellowish fog which swirled about her head and reduced visibility to no more than a few yards. The acrid taste of sulphur was in her mouth. She took shallow breaths at first and then great draughts of the foul air as her stride lengthened.

People were going home from work. She drew a few curious glances from those she overtook. Someone behind her stepped in a puddle and she heard a muttered curse. There was not a bus or a taxi to be had. She would have to walk all the way. Along the river to the Chelsea Embankment.

What would Donald think if he knew about this escapade? It wasn't the first time. There had been evenings when she could not face going home to that cramped little house. Donald, tired, taciturn, smoking. The smell of smoke got into the fabrics, the curtains and chairs. It hit you as soon as you opened the front door. She never lied to him. She simply said that she had to go up to town. Perhaps he believed that there was a late meeting at the Air Ministry and she had been asked to help. She would walk about the streets or sit in the corner of a pub sipping her drink. Sometimes the siren sounded and she had to run for an air-raid shelter. Then she would catch the last train back. Donald must be worried about her. She was worried about herself. How could she be so selfish, so inconsiderate, so cruel? In truth, she no longer recognised herself.

Perhaps that was what overwork did to one. She had not got the resilience, the emotional strength to discuss Johnny's death with Donald. Later. Not now. She did not trust herself to be sensible, to be kind and understanding or to talk about Johnny in a calm, rational way. Not yet. Later.

If she had a weakness, it was of the mind, not the body. She was driven by an almost demonic energy. The key to this mystery lay at the end of these dark streets. Why else should she feel herself drawn there with such speed, such certainty, like an iron filing rushing towards a magnet?

There was a light wind and in between sheets of fog, she caught a glimpse of the jagged silhouette of a bombed church outlined against the moon. She was close to the river now and here the fog clung to the arches of a bridge and draped itself about the buildings. In places there was a strong smell of burning where charred beams had been piled on top of the rubble that had been pushed to the side of the road.

A house rose up in front of her. This must be the place. A short flight of steps led to the door. Hanging from it was a notice. Bending down, she could just discern the words, 'The Fallen Angel. Members Only. Top Floor.'

The door opened to her touch. This did not surprise her. It was as inevitable as the sliver of light which beckoned to her from above. It was as inevitable as the sound of laughter that filtered down to her. The lower floors were in darkness but as she climbed she became conscious of a press of people around her.

'Let the lady through,' someone shouted. Another took her hand. He had dark, curly hair and a wide smile. 'I'm Mike. Mike Maguire.'

'Why are you out here?' she asked over her shoulder.

'We came out for a breath of air. Too many people inside.'

'Is Johnny there? Johnny Colgrave?'

'He should be. He came with us. Are you Johnny's girl?' He called up to Bill Lakin. '*Bill!* It's Johnny's girl! Get her a drink before she passes out.'

Lucy had the feeling of friendly hands helping her up the last flight towards the brilliant circle of light at the top.

Suddenly she felt faint and unsteady on her feet. A hand took her arm.

'Is that Chalky?' she whispered. 'Chalky White?'

'Why!' he exclaimed. 'Have we met?'

'In a way.'

'I'm admitting nothing,' he laughed. 'Not if you are Johnny's girl.'

'How do I find him?' She rested her head against the glass in the door but it was like stepping up to the moon. She could see nothing for the brightness.

'Just tap on the door and give it a push,' said Chalky.

And that is what Lucy did.

***

At the police station, Ron Lister was asked a lot of questions before he was allowed to go. 'She must have fallen fifty feet,' he said to anyone who would listen. 'I cannot remember when I was so upset. I waited outside the house. Anyone could see that the place had been bombed. I thought Mrs Tremlett would be out within a minute. Then I went inside and shone my torch around. The house was a shell. There was no roof. The staircase was still there but most of the floors had gone. Anyone who went up there must have been off their rocker. The last flight was no better than a diving board.

'And what is more…' he just stopped himself from saying worse, 'I don't expect to see a penny for this night's work.'

The Roman Road

It was a wild night, the wind ripping the last leaves from the trees and chasing a tumult of clouds across the merest sliver of a moon. A new moon seen through glass. Bad luck for some. He wouldn't have called himself a superstitious man, but on a night like this, disquiet found a darker, richer soil for its roots.

He shivered, taking a hand off the wheel to pull his jacket more tightly about him. The heater was old and defective. Switch it on and all you got was a puff of tepid air and a rattle from the fan. And the rattle wore on his nerves.

The lorry was being driven fast, too fast, but he was tired. He wanted to get home to Betty and see the boys before they were in bed. 'They are growing up so fast, Jim. They need you home more. I know we need the money, love, but they need a father. One day you will turn around and find it's all over. They have grown up and you've missed it.'

He ground his teeth, cursing the narrow road, the bare, whippy branches swinging at him, lashing the sides of the tarpaulin, the tortuous bends which pulled at the muscles in his shoulders, the sudden dips and hollows which waited for him like an ambush for soldiers separated from the column.

They were cruel, these long trips, but driving was the only trade he knew and he was too old to learn another. Fortunate to have a job at all the way things were going. How long had it been this time? Too long. Much too long. He yawned. He could tell you where he had been, reel off the names of the towns from the road signs like memorising a sequence of cards. That was a trick you used to see performed in the working men's clubs when he was a lad. Now all that the entertainer needed to do to raise a cheer was to drop his trousers.

Other people talked of travel. To him it was just distance. So many miles to be subdued, overcome, wrested from hill and valley and plain. Sometimes those miles came easy, unwinding their long grey ribbons, smooth as silk, yielding without a struggle. Sometimes they fought you every yard of the way, shook the bones in your body and the teeth in your head. Sometimes, when the sun came out after a shower of rain and the surfaces were like glass and you were on the home run, they wanted to dance with you. Take your partners for the last waltz.

Something caught his eye and he glanced in the wing mirror. The tarpaulin was bellying where a rope had worked loose. He swore softly. The road was bounded by tall beech trees whose shallow roots clutched at high banks on either side. The wind was still rising, the branches threshing in the half gale. He didn't want to stop. He was so close now. Just a mile or two to the old Roman road and there the country opened out and the road ran almost straight for ten miles. He would fix it then. He would be home within half an hour. Home ... home ... home...

The windscreen was misting up. He leaned forward and cleared a porthole in the cold pane. In the headlights the trunks of the trees seemed to rush at him as he went into the bends, as if a zoom lens had brought them into sharp focus.

Coming out of a corner he saw the lights of an approaching vehicle. Big, high-sided, cresting the switchback, running down the dip. He could see water lying in the hollow. He felt the brakes gently, trying to get a feel for the slippery surface, easing his foot back off the pedal as he sensed a slight loss of traction, concentrating on his steering. He was going to meet it all wrong. They would cross at the bottom of the slope. *The bastard*! Why didn't he pull over! He was right in the middle of the road! As he swung his wheel, the lorry swept past him in a flurry of noise and spray, drenching his windscreen, blinding him. *Hell*! He swiped at a lever to start the wipers going. For a split second he was steering by instinct. There was a heavy bump as if an inside wheel had caught the edge of a drain at the side of the road. The lorry lurched, corrected itself and regained the crown of the road as his windscreen cleared.

He slowed right down, bawling at himself for driving like a bloody learner, for turning a difficult situation into a dangerous one. The adrenalin pricked at his skin like heat rash. Slowly he felt the tension ebb from him, his grip on the wheel slacken, relieving his cramped fingers. He shrugged at his shirt, trying to lift it where it was clammy with sweat and sticking to his back. The trees were thinning. He was off the hill and onto the Levels. The Roman road stretched ahead of him, its poplars like twin files of soldiers. He pulled in and secured the tarpaulin. He drove gently now, paying out the extra minutes as cheerfully as if he was ransoming his life, as if it was the price of bringing him back safe and sound to those who loved him.

2

'Why didn't you bring your car, James? We could have had a girl each.' Ben glanced up at the passenger mirror watching for James to drop his jaw and his mouth to droop, a sign that he considered the question too banal to warrant a serious reply.

'Safety in numbers,' James replied.

They all laughed.

'Chicken,' said Louise.

'I think it's lovely,' Claire put in quickly. 'Us all being together like this. And all knowing each other. I've been to christenings where the godparents met for the first time in the church porch. Not very cosy.' After a moment of reflection, she added, 'I suppose it's because we are all friends of Nicola.'

'Brilliant,' said James cuttingly.

'God, you are odious sometimes!' Louise said. 'Why didn't you stay at home?'

'If Nicola had been married,' Ben said, 'I expect the proud father would have produced a couple of godparents.'

'Some girl he had been bonking witless for years and a mucker from university he gets legless with every Saturday night,' said James sourly. 'We're probably better off as we are.'

Louise turned to make huge eyes at Claire behind her. 'What a flatterer the man is.'

The car picked up speed as they left the village and turned onto the main road. 'It's a bit odd having a christening miles from where the mother lives,' said Ben.

James sniffed. 'I don't think it's at all odd under the circumstances.'

'I'm surprised you are allowed to have a christening at all so long after the happy event,' said Claire.

'The unhappy event,' James corrected her.

'You would think that the vicar would set some sort of time limit,' Claire went on a little breathlessly.

'I don't think it would be very Christian,' said James, 'to treat new babies like Beaujolais Nouveau. You can't just pour them down the drain after six months.'

'You would be surprised–' Ben began.

'Oh, Ben!' Claire protested. 'Don't be horrible. You men are spoiling everything. The little boy is sweet and Nicola is as proud as a peacock.'

'Peahen,' James quibbled. He was determined not to enter into the spirit of the occasion. He grudged any Saturday afternoon not spent browsing for bargains in some second-hand bookshop.

'Alright, a peahen,' Claire conceded sullenly.

Louise said, 'Do stop arguing. Gino is heavenly. Everything will turn out fine. You'll see.'

Ben swerved to avoid a fallen branch in the road. A blackbird skittered from a holly tree already bright with berries. 'You girls have seen Gino. Who does he take after?'

'He's a beautiful colour – not like us pasty-faced Brits. Glossy black hair and golden-brown skin – like a permanent suntan.' Claire ran a hand through her carroty hair. 'I'd swap my freckles for Gino's complexion any day.'

'The northern Italians are quite fair,' said Ben. He was driving slowly now, looking for a turning that would take them out of the gloom of the woods into the fitful sunshine.

'Not terribly relevant since Nicola's lover lives in Naples,' said James with a lawyer's relish for punishing a loose comment.

'Nicola's lover – you make it sound so coarse somehow,' said Louise.

'Well, wasn't it? He got her pregnant, scarpered back to Italy and hasn't been heard of since.'

'That isn't quite fair, James,' said Ben reprovingly. 'I'm sure they write to each other–'

'Nicola keeps his photograph next to her bed,' Claire broke in. 'She's obviously still crazy about him.'

'Got the hots for Sergio have you, Claire?' James taunted.

'No, I haven't!' Claire protested, her cheeks flaming.

'I think Nicola was very brave to have the child,' said Ben, who could be trusted to dispense conversational aspirins whenever the temperature started rising.

James ignored the prescription. 'What you really mean is that Nicola was off her head to want the baby and her parents should never have allowed her to have it.'

'You can't blame the parents,' said Claire. 'They didn't know until it was too late. Nicola told nobody. She kept it a secret until after her finals.'

'Nicola's crime was falling in love,' Louise said quietly. 'I don't mean the sort of tepid arrangement between couples who have done everything else except have a wedding. With Nicola and Sergio it was the real thing.'

'Tell us about "the real thing", Louise.' James caught Ben's eye and winked.

Louise fidgeted in her seat. 'You're just winding me up.'

'No, I'm not. I really want to know.' James sensed Louise's eyes on him and his face tightened in an effort to erase the mocking lines from his thin, sharp features.

'It's like two acrobats performing a once-in-a-lifetime act ... something that they cannot practise ... leaving the safety of the trapeze ... launching themselves into space ... knowing there can be no second chance ... daring the fates to come between them and bring them low.' She tossed her long dark hair, irritated with herself. 'It sounds so trite when you try to put it into words.'

'There are other ways.' James squeezed his hand between the car seats to rest it on her knee.

Louise smacked the hand lightly and swung her legs clear.

'Don't grope, James!' said Claire excitedly, moving her body a little closer to the danger zone. 'Go on, Louise.'

'You've made me shy,' Louise told her. 'Anyway, there isn't any more.'

James put on his most solemn expression. 'Go on. I promise not to tease.'

'Very few people have the courage to fall in love,' said Louise severely. 'Most of them just fake it – with the best of motives, of course. It makes their parents and their friends happy.'

This was too much for Claire. She was bouncing up and down in her seat. 'How could you say such a thing, Louise! I know people who fall in love all the time. Helen, my flatmate–'

'I can't see Helen as an acrobat,' said James. 'She hasn't the figure for it. I see her with baggy trousers and a bright-red nose throwing pails of whitewash all over the place.'

'Oh, James, how mean you are!' Claire subsided into reproachful silence.

Louise pressed her hand sympathetically. 'I don't see James launching himself into space. Not exactly a skydiver, are you, James?'

'I resent the suggestion that I'm some sort of emotional dwarf.'

Louise burst out laughing. 'You are too critical, James, too fastidious. If the Venus de Milo herself knocked on your bedroom door, you would stand her under a bright light and walk round and round her until you had found a chip in the marble and then send her back to her room.'

'Isn't she missing her arms?' said James.

'Oh, James! You're quite impossible!' Louise protested.

'I don't really see why James should have to defend himself.' Ben wound down the window and squinted at the sky. 'After all, he didn't get Nicola into this mess.'

'Here we go.' Louise nudged Claire with her elbow. 'The boys are closing ranks. We girls have a lot to learn about solidarity.'

'And about listening a little more and talking a little less.' Ben raised his eyes to the mirror, amused to see the girls turn to each other, rounding their eyes like children reprimanded in class.

'It's all very well Nicola and Sergio doing their circus act,' he persisted, 'but it has come unstuck and the people with their feet on the ground have to pick up the pieces. Nicola's parents must be worried sick. They aren't remotely well off.'

'I'm sure Sergio would help if he could,' said Claire. 'He's got his degree.'

'A poor second in Civil Engineering,' James countered.

'Nicola says he's got a job with a construction company,' said Claire loyally, 'and the firm has just won a big motorway contract.'

James sniffed. 'They live like gypsies moving from site to site and job to job. Sergio is probably dossing down in a caravan with six others. What sort of a life is that?'

'If two people love each other–'

'Oh, Louise!' Ben groaned, showing the first signs of irritation. 'Sergio has been back in Italy for over a year. He's not yet twenty-two and he's the youngest of five. His parents have a flat in the suburbs of Naples. They have very little money. It may be ten years before he is in a position to support a wife and child. However much he may want to help Nicola, he can't do it.'

'You make her sound so feeble,' said Louise. 'Women are much more independent these days. We could have a woman as prime minister this time next year.'

'I can't see Nicola as PM,' said Ben facetiously.

'Well, you must admit that she has put no pressure on Sergio or his family,' persisted Louise. 'She's been absolutely marvellous considering–'

'Considering there's nothing Sergio or his parents can do,' interposed James, his tone taking on an edge, 'I would say that Nicola was facing facts for the first time. Her parents have had to face them from day one.'

'It must be wonderful to be so sure of everything,' said Louise hotly. 'You sound just like my father.'

'I can live with that. I have a lot of respect for your father.'

'Face the facts!' Louise mimicked James's clipped manner of speaking. 'It's our parents' way of saying, "I didn't get away with it and you aren't going to either."'

'I don't think you are being honest, Louise,' James objected. 'If Nicola was your daughter–'

'Now then, gang, we're nearly there, let's not quarrel.' Ben looked up at the scudding clouds. 'You girls will have to hold on to your hats.'

Louise had found the road map in a side pocket. She flicked over the pages sightlessly, tears pricking at her eyes.

'Do you think Mr Channing will be there?' asked Claire, throwing a makeshift bridge across the awkward silence.

'I can't help noticing the way everyone calls him *Mister* Channing,' Ben remarked. 'It's never Edward Channing, let alone Edward.'

Claire squirmed. Her nose wrinkled with a fine distaste. 'He's so old and musty. Helen and I saw him at the library last Saturday. Ma was in bed with a beastly cold and she asked me to return a book for her. We had been shopping together – trying on hats and having complete hysterics–'

'Is there a point to this story? If so–'

'Oh, do shut up, James,' cried Louise, 'and let Claire finish.'

James sighed and stretched his legs resignedly while Claire went on. 'There was a queue at the counter in the library. Some old bat was bickering away at the assistant which set us off again. Mr Channing must have heard us because he came out of his office and–'

'I hope he chucked you out,' James grumbled.

'No, he was trying so hard to be friendly. That was what was so awful. He's so ... so untogether ... all gangling arms and legs like a deckchair that's got in a muddle. He came up and shook hands and took the book from me and said he would deal with it. And then, instead of saying goodbye, he stood there blinking at us out of those dreadful bifocals and smiling like he always does. It makes him look so long-suffering…'

'No doubt he was wondering what on earth he was going to say to two idiotic girls. I must admit, I feel for him.'

Claire hacked at James's ankle but otherwise ignored the interruption. 'His hair is going grey and he's got that frowsty black suit which looks as if it came from the dead man's shop.'

'The dead man's shop?' Ben frowned.

'You know,' Louise replied, 'it's at the far end of Silver Street. They do house clearances and there are always those ghastly clothes hanging outside.' She shivered. 'The suits are almost threadbare. Shiny with age, darned and re-darned at the knees and elbows –

always black or dark grey as if the owners had died and left their shadows behind.'

'God, you are morbid today, Louise.' James took a tendril of hair from behind her ear and gave it a gentle but reproving tug.

'You've got to give the man credit for perseverance,' said Ben. 'He's been chipping away at Nicola for months, driving her to the shops on Saturday afternoons, going for walks with her and the child.'

Claire pursed her lips. 'I think it is rather disgusting. He must be twice her age.'

'He's almost forty,' said Ben. 'He can't help that.'

'I'm sure he is very worthy. I know he's on the committee of this and the committee of that but somehow I can't bear to think of them ... together.' Claire turned around with a guilty start. Mr Channing was following at a discreet speed and distance in his venerable Morris Estate. 'It's pathetic how proud he is of that car of his – always polishing it and varnishing the woodwork. It must be as old as he is.'

'You can't help feeling rather sorry for him,' said James. 'Rattling around in a three-bedroomed house he saved up years to buy. I expect he's lonely.'

'But he will be fine now,' said Louise, her eyes flashing dangerously, 'now that he has added Nicola to his list of good works.'

Ben took a hand from the steering wheel, took off his glasses and folded them away in his breast pocket. 'I do think,' he said, 'that goodwill is sometimes rather undervalued. Mr Channing may be a little old-fashioned but that doesn't make him some sort of freak. The fact is that...' Louise had drawn a long breath and Ben hesitated but she remained silent and he continued.

'Nicola's father isn't very fit. It must be hard having to keep up that house and look after all of them just on a colonel's pension. If Nicola married Mr Channing, it would take an enormous strain off her parents.'

The car turned into a narrow lane. In front of them the ground rose steeply and they found themselves cutting across the side of a hill. It was grazing land and poor at that: featureless save for clumps of tussocky grass and a flock of forlorn-looking sheep sheltering behind an outcrop of rock. Below them were the Levels, low-lying country intersected with a network of narrow dykes and dotted with herds of cattle.

The old Roman road was a mile or so away and ran almost straight for ten more between wooded hills to the north and south. It was lined by tall poplars widely spaced like sentinels along its length, their bare branches like spearheads and seemingly unmoved by the wind.

The top of a tower showed above a bulge in the side of the hill and then a few seconds later they saw the church on the crest.

'Is that it?' Claire exclaimed, screwing up her eyes. 'It's tiny. It's more like a private chapel.'

'I expect we will just manage to fit in,' said James, adding for the benefit of Claire who was sometimes a little slow to catch on, 'all ten of us.'

'Early English,' said Ben. 'You see how it's rough hewn. It's built from local stone on the site of an old camp.' He waved at the rings stepped into the hillside. 'You can see where the entrenchments were.'

'I thought the sheep made those,' Claire giggled.

James snorted. 'Plodding round and round the church, I suppose, like the siege of Jericho.'

'Well, why not?'

The road ended with a five-bar gate and there were two cars already parked on the verge.

'Don't tell me. This is where we get out and walk,' Louise moaned. She reached for her hat. 'I've only got thin shoes.'

Ben parked the car and they assembled by the small swing gate. A steep path corkscrewed up the hill to the low, grey stone wall which bounded the churchyard. He shaded his eyes with his hand. 'There's someone up there…'

James hitched up his trousers before lifting his eyes from the squelchy ground at his feet. 'I think it's Nicola.'

Ben screwed up his eyes against the wind. 'Yes, and she's carrying Gino. You can tell by the way she is standing. What is she doing there by herself looking out across the Levels? She really is an extraordinary girl.'

'Let's wave to her,' Claire suggested.

'Just leave her alone,' said Louise quietly.

They started off up the path, the wind tugging at their clothes and mussing their hair. Claire lost her hat to a gust and chased after it as it cartwheeled down the hill the way they had come. It came to rest, its rim muddied, against a clump of gorse. She inspected it ruefully. The small party stopped to wait for her. 'I know I'm going to get hysterics,' she shouted back at them against the wind, 'I simply know it. I can feel it coming on.'

3

It was just before eleven o'clock that morning when
Alec Burgess, a reporter with the *Western Gazette*,
called in at the county town's police station. He pressed
a bell in the small reception area and the ponderous
figure of the duty sergeant appeared at the window. The
sergeant rested his arms on the counter. 'Oh, it's young
Alec, is it? I suppose you want to see PC Appleyard
and stop him getting on with his work too?' He was a
large, softly spoken man with heavy eyebrows which
seemed permanently raised as if an engrained
scepticism had fixed them halfway up his forehead.

'Is he back yet, Sergeant?'

'Yes. Five minutes ago.'

'Has he got the pathologist's report?'

'How should I know? I'm just the hall porter.' The
telephone rang. The sergeant sighed. "Push off, Alec,
there's a good lad, Room B13, halfway down the
corridor. Just a couple of minutes, mind, and don't–'

Burgess missed the rest as he hustled out of the
room, stopping at the vending machine to buy one cup
of coffee and invest in a second. He found the door and
tapped lightly before making his way up the room. The
offices, with their desks and wall charts and posters,
always reminded him of school. Two officers engrossed
in typing reports didn't even raise their heads as he
passed them.

Brian Appleyard was seated at a desk at the far end
of the room. With his black hair coming to a point on a
high, white forehead, there was something of the badger
about his appearance. A scar at the corner of his mouth
was the result of a rugby injury but it gave him a

slightly menacing air which was not without its uses in the more difficult aspects of his work.

'White and two sugars, if I remember right,' said the reporter, placing the steaming mug on the desk.

The scar hooked upwards in amusement. 'Come to trade, have you?' The policeman motioned to Burgess to take a chair, picked up a small transparent bag from a shelf behind him and emptied the contents between them. 'A safety razor, a road map, a tobacco pouch.' He reached into the pouch, retrieved a few grains and held his fingers to his nostrils. He sniffed disapprovingly, 'Not my mixture. A wallet,' he continued, 'containing a photograph of a young woman, probably about eighteen years old, a girlfriend maybe.' He pushed the photograph across the desk. Burgess picked up the print. The girl had long dark hair which fell to her shoulders. She would have been plain but for her dark eyes, which were somehow compelling and hinted at strong emotions.

'No? Not my type either,' said Appleyard taking back the photograph. 'She looks as if she would pull the communication cord the moment you put down your newspaper. We have a passport.' He flicked it open. 'Issued in Naples four years ago to one Sergio Torre, born in Naples. Profession ... student ... but that could be out of date ... aged eighteen at the time of issue.' He stared at the photograph. 'A good-looking boy. He doesn't look like that now, poor bugger.'

'Killed outright?'

Appleyard reached down to his feet and picked up a clear plastic water bottle. It was split from end to end. Crushed flat. 'He was probably carrying it in the pocket of his jacket.'

'Who found him?'

'A bloke driving a milk tanker at about five o'clock this morning. Phoned for the ambulance. Torre was taken to hospital. Pronounced dead on arrival. That's the standard phrase. Cheerful, isn't it?' Appleyard sipped at his coffee. 'But I think the report will show that it happened at about nine o'clock last night.'

'Knocked down by a car?'

'Something much bigger than that. Probably a lorry. I spent an hour at the site with the photographer. The road has no hard shoulder, just soggy piles of leaves blown up against the bank. There was no sign of heavy braking but there were tyre tracks six inches deep. If he was caught in that soft ground, he wouldn't have stood a chance.'

'You'll have your work cut out to find the driver.'

'I agree. That's where we may need some help from you.'

'Can you get him for dangerous driving?'

The policeman shrugged. 'Too early to say. It was a crazy place for anyone to be walking on a bloody awful night. He may have been trying to hitch a lift. I have a notion that he wasn't more than a few hours walk from his destination. He would probably have scrounged some food at a farm and dossed down in a barn for the night.'

'Do you think the driver fell asleep?'

Appleyard shook his head. 'I doubt it. Not on that bad stretch of road. He may have been dazzled by headlights coming at him. It's possible he didn't even know that he had hit anyone – and won't know till he gets out and checks the vehicle. Maybe not even then.'

'What's this?' Burgess reached across the desk and picked up a small white box. 'May I?' He took the policeman's little shrug for permission and lifted the lid. Inside there was a blue velvet bag with a drawstring.

'It's a St Christopher medallion. We found it at the bottom of his rucksack.'

The reporter held up the medallion to the light. 'Real gold by the look of it. You can see the hallmark.'

'St Christopher must have nodded off.'

'You can't blame St Christopher. You have to wear the medal around your neck.' He pointed to a map on the desk. 'Where do you think the chap was making for?'

Appleyard unfolded the map between them. It was badly stained and so torn at the folds that it was coming apart. 'It's much easier to say where he came from. He started here, just south of Rome.' With his finger he traced a line linking a series of circles that had been made in pencil. 'And came through Milan, Frankfurt, Dijon, Paris ... then on to Rouen and Cherbourg. Judging by the condition of his boots, he did more than his share of walking.' He tipped over a pair of boots by the table leg and pushed them towards his companion.

Burgess whistled tunelessly. The soles were worn down to the welts. 'I call that doing it the hard way. Did he have any money on him?'

'A few French and Italian coins. A pound or two in English money.'

Burgess pointed to a mark on the map. 'It looks as if he crossed the Channel here – at Weymouth.'

Appleyard drained his coffee. 'The pride of the force just about managed to work that out.'

Burgess flushed, his reddening cheeks pointing up the crinkly fair hair. 'Sorry, Brian. I'm not trying to teach you your business.'

'Tell me what he did after that – and I'll forgive you.' The policeman folded his arms on the desk. He arched his eyebrows challengingly.

Burgess stared down at the map. 'Now you'll get your own back. I suppose it's obvious. Staring me in the face?'

'I think so – but you tell me.'

'He carried no address on him? No telephone number?'

'Nothing that I have found.'

Burgess pulled the map closer. 'There's a line under this village. But it's a long way from the coast. It must be about sixty or seventy miles inland.'

'Go on.'

'There is only one other mark – a tiny circle close to the old Roman road. A church or maybe a chapel. It's in the middle of nowhere.' He looked up, his eyes lit with suppressed excitement. 'I think there's a story here, Brian.'

'I had a feeling you might say that.' He levelled a finger at the reporter. 'Now, Alec, if you and I are to stay friends, you can't go to press with any of this. Not a single line until the next of kin has been informed. We have to telephone the details through to the Italian Consulate in London. Then the deceased has to be formally identified – that's bound to take a few days. You ought to know that but I'm spelling it out to you.'

Burgess picked up the medallion, angling it at the light, running sun spots up and down the walls. 'Give me a break, Brian. I can't go back to my editor without so much as a snippet. I might as well go straight to the Jobcentre and sign on. If the Consulate gets its skates on, they can have the information in Naples by lunchtime. While the local *Carabinieri* dry the family's eyes, I can belt round the countryside and fill in the gaps. I could have my story filed by late afternoon.'

Appleyard cast his eyes over the figures of his colleagues. The chatter of the typewriters had slowed to a desultory tapping. Burgess followed his hopes down the long white scar. The officer leaned forward, splaying his fingers on the top of the desk to support his weight. 'You listen to me, Alec. I don't want to come on heavy, but if you push me, I'll see you never get past the front desk again. The family has to be told in the right way. That takes time. Sometimes I think you newspapermen are no better than vultures. Supposing it was your–'

'Alright, Brian,' Burgess raised his hands in a gesture of surrender, 'I'll hold on. I promise.' Rising to his feet, he put a tentative finger on a corner of the passport photograph. 'If I could run a copy of this –'

Appleyard dropped his fist like a mallet head. '*Cool it!* Wait till I give you the word, Alec – or you will be the next casualty.'

'I'll call in tomorrow – just to see how things stand.'

The policeman grinned. 'Let me know what time – I'll make sure I'm out.'

Alec Burgess made a quick calculation. That church. It wasn't really in the middle of nowhere. There was a network of muddy lanes to get through, but if he put his foot down, he could be there in a little over half an hour.

4

'Well, here we are,' said Barbara Ashton cheerfully, 'I will pull in behind the others.' She looked in the rear mirror as she switched off the engine. 'I don't see Mr Channing's car but of course we are a little early.'

Nicola's mother pushed up the cuff of her coat and checked her watch. 'I promised Nicola that I wouldn't be early. What can I be thinking about this morning!' She put a hand on her companion's arm. 'You don't mind if we sit in the car for a few minutes?'

'Of course not, Marion.' She unfastened the buttons of her overcoat and settled back in her seat. 'What an adventure this is! I never knew there was a church in this wilderness.'

'Nor I,' Marion replied with a short, humourless laugh, 'but one can usually trust Nicola to do things rather differently.' She started to open her spectacle case but changed her mind and snapped it shut.

Barbara wondered if Marion had seen Nicola. At that distance it was impossible to be sure. The church and the small figure high up on the shoulder of the hill stood out in black against the sky like an old-fashioned silhouette. It was as if the wind had leeched all colour from the day.

'It was good of you to come to my rescue, Barbara. Not the easiest of occasions.'

'My dear, what with Nicola taking the car and Ted being laid up, I couldn't stand by and see you marooned.'

'I could have gone with Nicola but I knew that she wanted to drive here with Gino – have him to herself.' She angled the mirror and checked her make-up. 'Just as I knew that Ted would wake up with a bad attack of sciatica – and keep to his bed for the day.'

'Oh, come now, Marion, aren't you being a little hard on him?'

Marion shook her head. 'I don't blame him. I know what he's going through. In some ways it's easier without him.' Her shoulders drooped and she folded her hands in her lap.

'Perhaps things would have been different if we had had more children, but we were stationed overseas for so many years – Cyprus, Borneo, Hong Kong, difficult postings, some of them – there was always this feeling of, "We'll sort our lives out when we get back home." And then, suddenly, you find it's too late and the years have run away from you.'

'But you probably had more time for each other, Marion, more fun together than the rest of us. There's always a balance in life. Children are so selfish. One can't blame them – it's the survival instinct. But give them an opening and they will take you over.' She laughed. 'And then they grow up and tell you that you are stifling them.'

'I don't think Nicola would accuse us of fencing her in. If anything, we gave her too much freedom.' Nicola's mother straightened the regimental brooch on the lapel of her grey flannel coat. 'Do you know, Barbara, I don't understand Nicola. I thought that the generation gap was something that happened to other families but I have discovered how exhausting it is and how painful, trying to relate to someone, communicate with someone who one feels does not trust one, who as fast as one builds bridges, knocks them down again. I have tried and I have failed. I don't think I have ever felt so inadequate.'

'It's the very last word I should use to describe—'

'It's the only one, I assure you. And it is very chastening.' She put a hand to the heavily permed grey hair. 'I have never worried unduly about what people thought of me. Not until now. I have always been happy, proud even, to be written off as the typical army wife. Stolid in my way, rather limited *but loyal to a fault.*'

'Not written off, surely, Marion?'

'Well, if people think of me like that, I'm not ashamed of it. Helping Ted with his career was a job I enjoyed. I think I was good at it.'

'I'm sure you were, Marion.'

'I can hear you smiling, Barbara. *Watch out!* I'm developing an ear in my old age.'

Barbara *was* smiling. She could never quite understand why people, who in the ordinary way wouldn't dream of discussing their problems, poured their hearts out to her. Perhaps it was something to do with her invincible cheerfulness, undimmed even after ascending the bathroom scales every morning. Perhaps it was because she listened carefully and said very little, long experience having taught her that with gentle prompting, people will usually give themselves the good advice for which they come to others.

'Were you and Ted separated from Nicola for long periods?' she asked.

'Yes. It was inevitable. It went with the job. She was here for nearly all her schooling but we tried to get her out to us for Christmas and the summer holidays. Even that wasn't always possible and she would have to stay on with my sister. But as Ted became more senior it became a little easier. He finished as a lieutenant-colonel, you know.'

'I can see that you and he made a good team.'

'I used to think so but when something like this happens...' There was a constriction in her throat and she couldn't go on.

Her companion turned to her anxiously. 'You mustn't blame yourself for what happened, Marion. Gino is a lovely child and Nicola has the character and the resolution to make a life for both of them.' She raised her eyes to the lonely figure up on the hill. There were no trees in the churchyard, nothing but a low, dry-stone wall to provide a little shelter from the wind.

'But when Nicola got into trouble she didn't come to us ... she didn't talk to us ... not until it was too late. I come back to that again and again. I try to get past it but it's as if there has been a rock fall and the road is blocked – I can't.'

'You mustn't let this come between you and Nicola. Isn't this the real test of your love for each other – that you can put that behind you and go on from here?'

Marion shook her head slowly, wearily. 'I don't know, Barbara. I don't know any more. There are other things besides love – things that are just as important, perhaps more important – like honesty. There is no trust between us. We live in the same house but we watch each other like suspicious neighbours. Every morning I listen for her, hear her creeping downstairs before Ted and I are about.

'She draws the curtains in the sitting room and sits by the window until she hears the postman. Then she opens the front door quietly and runs down to the gate to pick up the letters. When she turns, I hide behind my curtains in case she sees me. I don't mean to spy on her but I find myself behaving like her. She doesn't make her telephone calls from the house – she goes to the end of the street and rings from a public telephone box. When she comes back she goes straight up to her room as if she was frightened that I would stop her and question her. It makes for a horrible atmosphere in the house.'

'Do you think she is in touch with ... Sergio?'

'Of course I do. I resent his behaviour more than I can trust myself to say. But in his defence, I have to admit that Nicola landed him in a situation that he can never have bargained for.'

'When Sergio knew that Nicola was pregnant, did he–'

'I know what you are going to ask. Were both of them of the same mind – determined to have this child?' Marion stared bleakly through the window. 'I don't know, Barbara. Nicola won't talk about it. But the way she looks at me sometimes ... pityingly ... as if I couldn't begin to comprehend what it was that she and Sergio felt for each other.'

There was silence between the two women for some moments before Barbara spoke again. 'But you have tried to talk it through with Nicola – sympathetically?'

'Yes. I have tried. But it's pointless. That's what she tells me. "It's pointless, Mummy – you wouldn't understand." And, Barbara, the awful thing is that she may be right. Who am I to judge?' She snapped open the clasp on her bag and shook a cigarette into her hand,

'You don't mind? I have been trying to give it up but today has set me off again.'

Marion wound down the window to feel the cool air on her cheeks. 'Ted and I have not had a very ... physical sort of marriage. Things changed after Nicola was born ... I had to get up nights ... Ted needed his sleep ... it happened slowly, gradually ... sometimes when I think about it I feel sad. It does seem to me that we allowed something rather precious to slip out of our lives but...' For a moment she was unable to continue and Barbara rested a hand on her arm.

'This is distressing you, Marion, you mustn't–'

'*I must, I must* ... I can't tell you what it's like living with your own thoughts going round and round and round like smoke that is trapped in a room and can't get out.'

'Marion, my dear...' Barbara pressed her hand gently. 'I should have done more. You must think me a very poor friend.'

Marion shook her head. 'You have nothing to reproach yourself for.' She took a deep breath and exhaled it slowly. 'It may sound strange to you, Barbara, but friendship is something I have never found easy. I am impatient with people who are incompetent and disorganised, whose lives are untidy, people who are always trying to extricate themselves from some tangle or other – but I notice that they are the ones who have all the friends.' She leaned forward and pulled open the ashtray under the dashboard. 'I used to believe that self-reliance was a virtue, but it often brings loneliness and that is a high price to pay.' She looked at her watch. 'Should we not–?'

'Yes, we must go.'

Marion nodded but she was only half listening. She smoothed her skirt in an abstracted way. 'It has been an anxious time. One cannot live on love – even Nicola's prodigious version of it. Unfortunately it doesn't pay the bills.'

Barbara fastened the buttons of her overcoat. 'It must be very worrying. Is there any hope of Sergio or his family being able to make a contribution?'

'None. I doubt whether Sergio can do more than feed himself and keep a roof over his head. His parents have no money – he cannot look to them. He must stand on his own feet now. All I ask is that he stays out of Nicola's life since he can do nothing for her – and gives her a chance to salvage something from all this.'

'And Mr Channing? I don't want to pry, Marion, but–'

'Will the knight come galloping to the rescue?' A hint of humour glinted from her eyes. 'I must say, Mr Channing makes a rather improbable St George.' She drew deeply on her cigarette and stubbed it out half smoked. 'Nicola has thrown away the sort of life we wanted for her, the sort of life she would have wanted for herself when she is older. Edward Channing seems to me the best that Nicola – or any of us – can hope for.' Across her wide cheekbones the skin seemed to slacken like a tent in the process of being folded. She reached into her coat for a shawl and tied it around her head. 'I didn't think it was a day for hats,' she said, pushing open the car door.

Together they walked through the swing gate. 'Do you want to take my arm, Marion?' asked Barbara. 'I had no idea it was blowing so hard.'

Marion seemed not to have heard the question. She walked slowly up the path, her head down. 'It probably sounds ridiculously old-fashioned, Barbara, but I would like to know – do you think that Edward Channing is a good man?'

'I think he is a kind man. I believe he loves Nicola.' The wind made little rushes at them, nudging them, buffeting them as if they had been caught up in a throng of mischievous children. 'Do you think that Nicola is being ... quite fair to him?'

'I have told Nicola that she cannot go on exploiting Edward, treating him like some sort of unpaid servant and buckshee chauffeur. I'm sure he does loves her in his way and he adores the child.'

'He has helped her over a very difficult time. Whatever one may–'

'Edward is the last person I ever expected to entertain as a prospective son-in-law but it breaks my heart to see him turning up at the house on Saturday afternoons in his best suit, all brushed and polished and ... Nicola so cold towards him ... so disdainful. I tell you, Barbara, sometimes I feel like picking her up and shaking her, telling her that she doesn't deserve him, that she should go down on her knees and thank God he is prepared to take on the pair of them.'

They could see Nicola quite clearly now. She was very pale, impassive, expressionless, her head to the wind, her dark hair streaming behind her, still looking out over the Levels, the child motionless in her arms.

In some places steps had been cut, shored up with lengths of rotting wood; in others it was little better than a muddy track. Marion raised her head to wave at the small group of people fretting, it seemed to her, under the porch. Someone waved back. She paused for breath. 'Ted was so proud of Nicola. He had this little dream that she would marry into his regiment. When I think of the trouble he went to – arranging tennis parties in the summer, getting the young officers over from the depot, jugs of Pimms on the lawn, Ted in his best blazer ... all that effort over that withdrawn, rather ordinary girl ... oh, Barbara,' she gave a little gasp and the wind swept a tear from the corner of her eye, 'it was so transparent, so futile and, if you think about it, so very, very funny.'

Barbara gave her companion an anxious look and would have taken her arm but they both turned at the sound of a car approaching.

'That will be Edward,' said Marion.

There was something in her voice which Barbara could not let pass. 'Have you and Nicola made a decision?'

'We have reached ... an understanding. Edward called round last night. He asked if he could talk to Ted and me in private. Things were obviously coming to a head. I had to temporise. I asked him to come to tea next weekend. I couldn't tell him anything. When he had left, Nicola confronted me. She had overheard part of the conversation. She said that I had no business to interfere in her life. I told her that Ted and I would do what we could to help her but that all the fantasising about Sergio had to stop. I was very firm with her. I said that things were very difficult and she should think seriously about accepting love and support where it was offered. She couldn't have it both ways. It wasn't fair on Edward. He had to know where he stood. She made me promise to wait until after the christening. I told her that she was being absurd.'

Edward Channing emerged from his car. He bent down and straightened his tie in the wing mirror. 'Don't you think that we should wait for him?' Barbara suggested.

They took a few steps off the path and stood in the lee of a large rock while Mr Channing made his way up the hill towards them.

Marion pointed to the solitary figure standing in the corner of the churchyard. 'Look at her, Barbara. That's just the way she looked. I said that we quarrelled but I was the one who was upset. Nicola was very composed. She has this way with her. As if she knows more than she's telling, which I find so irritating. She might have been the queen herself the way she faced me. Standing very erect ... her chin held high ... not insolent but ... but proud. Do you know what she said, Barbara?' Nicola's mother closed her eyes and her lips moved silently as she recited to herself. 'She said, "I will marry the man who stands beside me tomorrow." Of course it was preposterous but she spoke the words as she would her marriage vows.'

Barbara's attention was distracted by Mr Channing calling to them. 'I do believe Edward Channing has bought himself a new suit, Marion. And look at that bunch of daffodils he is carrying.' There was colour in his cheeks and a light in his eye. 'Look at him now – waving at Nicola. Trying to get her to turn her head.'

A cry from Nicola was borne to them on the wind. It seemed to eddy around their heads and then fade slowly as if a horseman had shouted over his shoulder before riding away. Nicola cried out again and now they saw her run through the lychgate to the shoulder of the hill. As she stood there looking out over the Levels, shading her eyes with her free hand, the church clock tolled the hour. It was exactly midday.

A narrow shaft of sunlight sliced through the clouds. It was so unexpected that the two women turned from watching her to follow the direction of her arm. The Roman road shone as if the blade of a sword had been laid flat along its length. A shadow hurried along the road and when it came abreast of them, changed direction, flitting towards them over the flat fields and watercourses. The shadow of a man. A man running. Then the clouds closed over once more.

A Sense of Obligation

I used to see Arthur once a year, always in the first
week in December, when he came up to London to do
his Christmas shopping. We had both retired from the
City after the Stock Exchange moved over to electronic
trading. Of course, the bowler hats and rolled umbrellas
went years before that but he and I always wore a
bowler. We didn't feel dressed without it. Old habits
die hard.

We always met at midday and at the same public
house a short walk from Liverpool Street Station. The
bar was tucked away in the basement of an old building
among a maze of alleys that had escaped Hitler's
attentions. You could smell the beer as you descended
the flight of stone steps and at the bottom there were
rows of beer barrels, stacked one upon another, and
sawdust on the floor to mop up the spillages.

Arthur was always out of breath when he arrived.
He was overweight and puffing and his cheeks went in
and out like a pair of pink balloons. We sat on bar
stools and knocked the same old reminiscences back
and forth, prompting each other when memory failed
and laughing as hard as if we were hearing them for the
very first time.

We had worked in the same stock-broking firm for
ten years and then Arthur moved to Wexlers, the
merchant bank, but he didn't stay long. He reminded
me of my first few weeks with the stockbrokers. I was
in the general office and it was my first real job.

Whenever a piece of paper that I did not
understand appeared on my desk – and there were many

of them – I was too timid to seek advice and simply crumpled it up into a tiny ball and placed it in the waste-paper basket. 'Within a month, the administration of the firm had sunk into chaos!' Arthur guffawed, wiping his mouth with the back of his hand. 'You were lucky not to have been sacked!'

Then there was old Herbert. He worked with the firm's dealers in the 'Box', a small outpost close to the floor of the Exchange. This is where we took the orders from the partners to buy or sell stocks and shares for clients. Arthur was a Blue Button. His job was to record the changes in the prices of the most important shares every hour and telephone them to the main office.

'Herbert had been a fireman during the Blitz,' Arthur recalled. 'The poor devil was hit on the head by a piece of falling masonry. Ninety-nine days out of a hundred, he was as right as rain but once in a while he would have one of his turns. His face would go very white and he would brush his moustache between finger and thumb and stride onto the trading floor as if he owned it. Herb would march up to the jobbers and buy or sell a million pounds worth of stock. Without instructions! Bargains were struck verbally in those days but–'

'They had the force of Holy Writ,' I added, coming in on cue.

'That's right.' Arthur nodded solemnly. 'The jobbers could have insisted that we honoured the contract but they knew Herb's little quirks and they always cancelled the deal.'

One story followed another and so did the pints of ale. Punctually at one, we went off to a small restaurant that we had used for years. In the old days you could have soup, bangers and mash and then apple pie and custard for a few shillings.

The menu was much the same but the prices made me blink and reach for my glasses. 'Arthur,' I said, as I speared a Cumbrian sausage, 'do you remember Ned?'

'*Do I remember Ned?*' Arthur's broad shoulders started to shake. 'The funny thing about Ned was that he was born without an ounce of ambition.'

Ned joined the firm just after the war. He was quite well connected and brought in just enough business to keep his job. 'At two o'clock in the afternoon, regular as clockwork,' I said, 'Ned would come back from lunch, sit at his desk and snap his fingers at the clerk in the desk behind him.'

'Sometimes that was me,' Arthur chuckled. 'I had to wake him up when the partners came back from their lunch. That was about four o'clock if they had downed a second glass of port. I used to tie a thread of cotton around his little finger and give it a tug when I heard them coming up the stairs.' And we laughed and laughed and then the sight of each other's faces would set us off again.

We left the restaurant and, as always, we did not take the shortest way back to the underground station but walked a little out of our way so that Arthur could buy a copy of the *Evening Standard* from the newspaper seller on the corner of Cannon Street.

The man was sitting on an upturned orange box with a pile of newspapers on a makeshift table. His coat was worn but his shoes were polished and he held a woollen scarf tightly against his throat. At the sight of Arthur he raised a pair of bushy grey eyebrows and forced his pinched features into something like a smile.

'Hello Steffen!' Arthur took his hand. 'How is life treating you?'

'Not badly,' the man replied. He started to cough. 'Not badly at all.'

Arthur took a paper. 'Steffen, promise me you will let me know if there is anything I can do to help?'

'Of course. Thank you.' With some difficulty, his fingers closed around the coin and he dropped it into a tin. 'I promise.' This brought on a violent fit of coughing and he waved us away.

'I never told you about Steffen,' said Arthur, 'but I have a feeling that he won't be there next Christmas and I would like to think that someone else remembers him when he is gone.'

'Tell me,' I said.

'Steffen and I shared an office at Wexlers,' Arthur began. 'They were old-established bankers that had been owned and run by the Wexler family for many generations. I was lucky to get taken on. Times were hard. The partners had gone without pay for twelve months and the rest of us suffered big cuts in salary. We had recently had an addition to the family and we were digging into our savings.

'I heard that Wexlers were replacing someone in their investment department and I applied for the job. I was interviewed by the boss, Horst Wexler himself. He was a tall, slim, sallow-faced man who rarely smiled. He was a legend in the City, a man who could break a company's reputation with a shake of his head.

'I was very nervous but he did his best to put me at my ease. What impressed me was how much he already knew about me. He even knew the name we had christened the new baby. He asked me what qualities I regarded as the most important in an employee. I stammered something about honesty and a capacity for hard work.

'He took those for granted, he told me. Loyalty was the quality he prized the most. Remember that, he said. If you join Wexlers, he said, you will be part of a big family.

'Well, to cut a long story short, I landed the job. I made friends and got to know a bit about the people who worked in the firm. The thing that struck me as remarkable was how much each of them owed to Horst Wexler.

'Take Steffen, for instance. He had been brought up in Germany. His family had built up a prosperous business in Dortmund but they were ruined by the collapse of the currency. When Wexler found him he was almost destitute. He brought him to London and within ten years he was running a department at the bank.

'Steffen owed that man everything. I could tell you a dozen similar stories of people who worked in that bank.' We crossed the road and Arthur took my arm and we stopped on the edge of the pavement.

'Horst had a son, his only child. He was called Klaus. He was at public school. A fine looking boy, clever and a good games player – in fact, he was everything that his parents could have wished for. It was no secret that one day he would step into his father's shoes.

'Then a tragedy occurred. Klaus caught poliomyelitis and died. Those were the days before the discovery of the vaccine. It happened just before Christmas. We were all prepared for the annual office party to be cancelled but Mr Wexler insisted that it went ahead as usual.

'He was a man who never touched alcohol but in the course of a couple of hours he drank quite a lot. It was about seven o'clock in the evening, and dark and raining hard when the party ended. Mr Wexler left the building, placed his black Homburg on his head, hoisted an umbrella and started for home. Steffen and I were heading for the underground station and were a few paces behind him.

'Mr Wexler had given his chauffeur the afternoon off and he hailed a cab. It stopped on the other side of the road and he signalled to it to stay there. The road was clear as he stepped off the pavement.' Arthur pointed to his feet, 'It happened just here.

'A delivery van came around the corner. It was being driven much too fast. The driver slammed on the brakes and the van skidded in the wet without losing speed. Mr Wexler may have been unsighted by his umbrella or, perhaps, it was the effect of the drink but he didn't move nearly quickly enough to save himself.

'Steffen leaped into the road, grabbed Mr Wexler by the shoulders and pulled him out of the way of the van. They both fell in a heap in the gutter. Mr Wexler picked himself up and helped Steffen to his feet.

'He was very shaken. So was I. Of course I make full allowance for the tragedy that he had suffered but, to us, Mr Wexler was a god-like figure, a man of enormous riches, a man who was always completely in command of himself, a man who did not, it seemed, need other people. Yet, in the space of an hour or two, I had seen him partly incapacitated by drink and escape death by inches thanks only to the presence of mind of one of his clerks.'

Arthur and I parted at the underground station. 'Mr Wexler sacked us both the next day,' he said, 'and without a word of explanation.'

'From Mount Olympus to the gutter,' I murmured, 'and all in the space of a few seconds.'

Arthur frowned. 'That's a bit high flown for me,' he said. 'Anyway, he gave us a month's salary. I found another job but poor Steffen simply went to pieces. Eventually, he got a part-time job with the *Evening Standard* and he has been there ever since.' He raised his bowler. 'I hope we shall meet again next year.'

High Stakes

For Captain Derek Headland, it had been a difficult evening. He had lost heavily at the tables and had been refused any more credit. To heap indignity upon indignity he, a British officer, had then been summoned by the manager.

The room was cramped and very warm. The fan in the ceiling turned slowly, hardly stirring the air. Bin Khouri, a large man in a white sharkskin suit, was sitting behind his desk. Derek was halfway into an armchair when Bin Khouri snapped his gold-ringed fingers and directed him to the hard chair in front of him, as if he was a clerk at a job interview.

The manager smiled, revealing several gold teeth. 'I am desolated that we cannot accommodate you any further. I have to answer to the proprietors and although they are rich men, they have not got limitless funds.'

Derek sniffed. 'I would have thought that five thousand pounds was a drop in the ocean to them.'

'Perhaps, but you are not our only creditor.' His fingers drummed on the top of the desk. 'You will have to find the money, my friend, and find it soon.'

Derek's shirt was clammy and sticking to his back. Small rivulets of sweat ran down the inside of his arms. He wanted to bawl at the man that he was a shyster who should be run out of town but he forced himself to keep his temper. 'That will not be a problem.' He pulled an engraved silver case from his pocket, tapped a cigarette into his hand and lit up.

'It makes me very happy to hear you say so. May I ask how you will obtain the money?'

'I have substantial funds in London. I will have the money wired to Cairo.'

'And when may I expect to have it in my hand?' The words slithered off Bin Khouri's tongue like a snake moving through grass.

'Soon. Very soon.' Derek tugged at his tie. The heat in the room was intolerable.

'How will that be, Captain Headland? Your leave finishes tonight. Tomorrow you must return to your regiment.'

Rage and frustration, fuelled by bad cards, cheap whisky and the man's persistent needling, washed over Headland. *'Don't push me, Bin Khouri!'* he shouted. 'I have only to pick up the telephone to have this rats' nest closed down.'

'But I do not think that you will do that, my good friend.' Bin Khouri leaned over the desk, his smile broadening. 'The Anubis Club is off limits to British Army personnel. A perverse and misguided regulation in my opinion but, for the moment, we are not our own masters. How would you explain your presence here tonight?'

Derek raised himself out of his chair. It would do no good to quarrel with the man. He had powerful friends and spies everywhere. 'I'm sorry,' he said. 'It's the heat. I did not mean to be uncivil.'

Bin Khouri waved a hand. 'No hard feelings, Captain. Perhaps you would like to refresh yourself before you leave. There is a hammam behind the club and if you require any further relaxation, we can offer … other distractions.'

'I know about your other distractions,' Derek forced a smile.

'Ah,' Bin Khouri rose to his feet. 'I was forgetting the beautiful Leah. She will be sad not to see you tonight.'

'You will have to remind her that there is a war on and some of us have to fight.' He swayed and held on to the door for support.

'Let me call a taxi. You should not drive yourself after such a tiring evening.'

'My jeep is parked round the back. Don't worry. I can look after myself.'

'I am sure you can. We will go to the back door.' Bin Khouri drew in a draught of the night air as he watched Derek clamber into the vehicle. 'I look forward to settling everything on your next leave. You will be sure to visit me? I should be very disappointed not to see you.'

Derek grunted a reply and pressed the starting button. As he pulled away, he had the disquieting feeling that he had been observed. There had been another car parked some ten yards behind his jeep. Had it been empty, he would have been able to look straight through it to the blue glow cast by the neon lights. But there was something or someone in the way.

He drove slowly. He did not want to be stopped by the military police and asked a lot of awkward questions. The moonlight turned the walls of the houses a ghostly white and cast blue shadows across the alleys. He passed the myriad dwellings that made up the necropolis, the city of the dead. Their troubles were behind them. He felt a pang of envy. They did not have to worry about the Bin Khouris of this world.

How different things would have been if he had been the elder son. But for an accident of birth, he would stand to inherit a large estate when his father died – a big house, several thousand acres of farmland and some of the best shooting in the West Country.

What would his father leave him? Fifty thousand pounds, perhaps. By no means a negligible sum but a pittance compared with what Harry would get. An accident of birth.

His elder brother was in the same battalion and they were in the middle of a war. An accident could happen at any time. Harry was married but, mercifully, there were no children. No son and heir. Not yet. In his billet, lying under a single sheet, his thoughts took an ugly turn. He pushed them away but they came back and the sky was getting light before at last he slept.

Two days later, Derek had rejoined his unit in the desert some two hundred miles west of Cairo. He had written a letter to his father, Sir Thomas Headland, DSO. He hoped that he would never have to write another like it. He dared not risk it coming into the hands of his commanding officer who routinely censored the officers' letters so he had sent it with a friend returning to England on leave with instructions to post it on arrival.

The following afternoon, Derek and Harry were each in command of a troop of armoured cars on a reconnaissance patrol. German tanks and aircraft had been reported in the area and Derek should have been giving his full concentration to the task of keeping a lookout.

But the words of that letter were still going around his head. He had told his father that he needed an advance on his inheritance. He must have five thousand pounds – and quickly. Then he had lied. It was a debt to a brother officer. A debt of honour. Of course he knew that gambling was forbidden in the regiment but, on a dinner night, after the port had circulated, things sometimes got out of hand.

In that letter, he swore a solemn oath never to gamble again. He hinted at the disgrace that reneging on the debt would bring. He said nothing about Bin Khouri or the Anubis Club. Naturally, his father would be very upset. 'Colonel Tom' had commanded the same mob in The Great War. It was like a second family to him. He might have to sell a farm but he would raise the money rather than see his son drummed out of his regiment.

Derek heard them before he saw them. That unmistakeable, ear-splitting scream. *'Stukas!'* someone yelled, but it was already too late. The bombers caught them too closely grouped in a shallow bowl of sand hills.

Everyone dived out of the cars. Seconds later, smoke and flame, mangled metal and charred bodies lay strewn across the desert. Harry and Derek and Paddy, his troop sergeant, were the only survivors. The three of them were suffering from burns but Paddy had a serious shrapnel wound in the stomach and was losing blood fast. Petrol cans were exploding and they dragged the wounded man out of range.

Harry crouched down beside him and tried to stem the flow but with little success. The sergeant's face was white with pain. 'Leave me here, Sir,' he pleaded, 'and save yourselves. I'm finished.'

'Nonsense, Paddy. Hang on. We will get you back to base and fix you up.'

Derek limped up to the top of the sand dunes and put his field glasses to his eyes. 'Of all the infernal luck,' he muttered. 'There's a German column,' he shouted to his brother. 'Now it has halted. They must have spotted all this smoke. A half-track is peeling off. It's turning this way.'

'How long until it gets here?' Harry called back.

'Fifteen minutes. Maybe less.' Derek slid down the slope to rejoin his brother. Every nerve in his body was twitching, telling him to be gone. 'You can't do anything for Paddy. He's had it.'

Harry glared at him. 'I'm not leaving Paddy. Not like this. We have been together since Dunkirk.'

'He will be dead within the hour.'

'You don't know that.'

'Then we take him with us.' A germ of an idea was sprouting in Derek's mind.

Harry scanned the crest of the dunes behind him. 'We would have to carry him up that slope and be out of sight before Jerry spots us. There isn't time. The only chance of saving his life is to give ourselves up. Throw down our arms in full view of the Germans.'

'So, Paddy dies in a couple of hours and you and I spend the rest of the war in the bag.'

'I hate the idea of surrendering but Paddy could be in a dressing station within the hour and a field hospital later tonight. He could pull through.'

'Look at him, Harry. He's lost too much blood. Think of it. Three years in some lousy camp. Perhaps four. When we should be fighting for our country.'

'I'm the senior captain. Either he comes with us or we stay here and surrender. That's an order.'

'Alright. We will take him. The light is going. Ten minutes should see us over that ridge. In half an hour it will be dark.' He patted his pocket. 'As soon as Jerry has gone home, we will send up a flare.'

'*A flare!* Good for you. That might just save our bacon.'

Derek took Paddy's arms and Harry grabbed his legs. The two men staggered up the slope with their burden. The sun was sinking and their shadows stretched out in front of them.

'Are you sure about that ten minutes?' gasped Harry. 'That half-track sounds bloody close.'

If Derek replied, Harry never heard the answer. They were a few yards from the top when the Germans opened fire. Harry was hit immediately and rolled down to the bottom. Paddy was already dead. Derek dropped him and scrambled over the crest and ran for his life.

The men in the half-track had plenty to occupy them and did not come after him. He spent the night in a dry river bed and, at first light, started walking back to the Allied lines. The flare was damaged and didn't light but he did have a compass and early that afternoon he was seen by a patrol and driven back to his unit.

Derek received a cool welcome from his comrades. The Intelligence Officer had some information about Harry. He had been taken prisoner but he had been hit in the spine and would probably never walk again. Only Derek had returned. Derek almost felt that he should apologise for being alive.

A few days later he received a letter from his father. It was very cold. One of the farms would have to be sold to raise the sum required. That would take at least three months. The chap to whom he owed the money would have to be patient.

The only cheering news, his father added, was that Harry would qualify for exchange with a badly injured German POW and might be home soon. 'I must warn you,' the letter concluded, 'that Harry will have to be nursed for the rest of his days. I had hoped to leave you some money when I die but your brother's needs must take priority. I am altering my will to take account of the new situation.'

Derek had been given leave to spend the weekend in Cairo. He sent a message to Bin Khouri assuring him that he would get his money but telling him that he would have to wait a few weeks for it.

On the Friday morning he was told to report to the office of his CO, Lieutenant Colonel Douglas Fortescue. He guessed that it was probably some news about Harry. He opened the door and saluted smartly. The Colonel was tall with sandy hair and a neat moustache. He had won two DSOs in the desert and was resisting transfer to the staff of divisional headquarters although it would bring immediate promotion.

He usually had a ready smile but he was looking very grim. Standing at his side, his face expressionless, was Captain Gerard Vaux, an officer in the Intelligence Corps.

'I want to keep this meeting very short,' said Fortescue. 'I must inform you that the Anubis Club has been closed down. The tables were fixed. Gamblers who lost more than they could afford laid themselves open to blackmail and we have had reports that the manager was selling details of Allied troop movements to the Germans.'

Derek felt the blood drain from his face. 'No doubt this action was not taken without careful consideration, Colonel.' He cleared his throat, 'But I am not sure what it has to do with me.'

'It has this to do with you,' said the Colonel. He pushed a piece of paper across the table. It was a statement signed by Bin Khouri listing the dates on which Derek had visited the club, setting out the total of his losses and demanding that his commanding officer put pressure on him to settle his debts.

'Do you deny any of this?' the Colonel inquired. 'Before you answer, I should warn you that you were seen leaving the club by two officers in the Intelligence Corps.'

Derek lowered his eyes. Now this. Just when he thought things could not get any worse. 'I cannot deny it. But Bin Khouri has sent this demand in retaliation for the closing of the club. He is furious and intends to cause us the maximum embarrassment.'

'He has succeeded,' the Colonel commented dryly.

'He would have been paid in full within three months. My father –'

'*You mean to tell me that Colonel Tom knows about this!*' The CO removed his spectacles and they clattered down on the table. 'I suppose you told him that you owed money to a brother officer?'

Derek's silence answered for him.

'It was not enough to disgrace yourself,' the Colonel pursued, 'you had to disgrace your regiment.'

'I had to put it like that,' Derek muttered. 'It was my only way out.'

'That is where you are wrong,' said the Colonel. He pushed back his chair. 'There is another way out, Captain Headland, and that is out of this regiment – *at once and as far from the rest of us as possible!* West Africa is in my mind. Go to Cairo and stay there until your posting comes through. This meeting is at an end.'

In Cairo, Derek sat at a bar, sank another scotch and brooded over the day. The humiliation did not end in the Colonel's office. He was escorted to the camp perimeter where he waited in the sweltering sun, attracting curious glances, until a car could be found.

By now the story would be all round the regiment. In a week it would be all round the county. West Africa. That wouldn't suit him at all. That wasn't his style. But no more was settling down in some suburban villa after the war and trimming his champagne tastes to a beer income.

Some chaps would find a quiet spot and blow their brains out. But he had always been a gambler. The odds were unattractive but he had been in tighter corners before and come out on top. He could feel the adrenalin coursing through him. He wasn't playing with chips this time. His life was the wager. Living, breathing, nerve and sinew. Flesh and blood, bone and muscle pitted against the ambition of the knife, the gun, the club or the garrotte. It was terrifying. And exhilarating. His fingers curled around the grip of his service revolver. Never had he felt so truly alive as he did at that moment.

For the next two hours he trawled the Arab bars in the sleazier parts of the city. He went on drinking and he told anyone who would listen what he would do to Bin Khouri when he found him.

The man's spies slipped away, reported to their master and received their orders. The following morning, the body of Derek Headland was found in a corner of the necropolis. His throat had been cut. There were rumours that he had taken three of his assassins with him but nothing was ever proved.

Anyone for Tennis ?

The market stallholders called her Magpie Maggie. She liked shiny objects and that beady eye of hers rarely missed a bargain. She married during the war but things did not work out and she had to find some means of earning a living. Like the rest of us, she made some bad mistakes while she was learning but before very long she built up a nice little business visiting out-of-the-way houses where the owners were usually elderly and wished to dispose of the odd piece of silver or an unwanted table or chair to help make ends meet.

The war made me a widow and there were no children, so when I had finished moping I took over a lease in what had formerly been a large shop but had been subdivided into boutiques and I started dealing in second-hand furniture. It made a small profit and my neighbours were a friendly lot and the days passed pleasantly enough.

One Monday morning, Maggie arrived in her Mini van and parked in a side street. I asked someone to keep an eye on my shop while I returned with her to look at her latest purchases. There was a nice Victorian screen and we argued amicably before settling on a price.

Maggie was not her usual ebullient self. She looked rather wan and seemed subdued so I took her to the corner shop and bought her a cup of coffee. 'Something is on your mind,' I said. 'You can tell me off for being nosey. I shall not be hurt.'

She gave me a rueful smile. 'I would probably have told you anyway.' Something rather strange, rather unsettling, had happened the previous Saturday.

'I regularly place small classified advertisements in the newspapers under a box number and I received a reply from a Mrs Hazelrigg.

'The handwriting was that of an elderly person. The letters were spidery and written in violet ink. She said that she and her sister, Edith, had some old silver that they rarely used and if I was interested, I should telephone and make an appointment. She signed herself Eleanor Hazelrigg.

'When I called, it was she who answered the telephone. She spoke in a thin, reedy voice which kept sinking to a whisper as if she was afraid of being overheard. "If it wouldn't be too much trouble," she said, "drive over and have a look at it and see what you think. We can have an early cup of tea."

'It was a very warm day and I had the window wound right down. I took it fairly slowly and had to stop more than once to look at my map. At last, I was driving down a sandy track which seemed to lead nowhere when I came to a rambling, red-brick house in a clearing of tall trees.

'The front door had a glazed panel typical of the period. On the brickwork to one side, the name of the house was shown as "Aruana". I pressed the bell and waited but no one came to the door so I walked around the back.

'Almost covered by a tangle of overgrown creepers, was a greenhouse. I have always been interested in plants and I could not resist pushing on the door. It opened just enough to permit me to put my head in, but no more. There was a tall, spiky plant with a purple flower which I did not recognise. It gave off a peculiar scent and within a few moments I felt very unsteady and had to leave quickly.

'I closed the door behind me and drew in great draughts of fresh air until my head was clearer. In front of me the ground sloped down quite sharply. Steps descended to a flat lawn which was obviously used as a tennis court for the net and net posts were still in place, the grass was neatly trimmed and the white markings looked quite fresh.

'What need of a tennis court had two elderly ladies? I could only assume that they had younger friends who used it. Beyond it lay a meadow and a stream and then a hillside, heavily wooded and with no evidence of another dwelling.

'Behind me, a glass conservatory ran most of the length of the house. It was impossible to see inside for the blinds had been pulled down. I tapped on the door. Again there was no answer. I knocked again, this time louder. Nobody came. Irritated and still feeling rather muzzy, I found a pair of wooden seed boxes and stood on them.

'By craning my neck, I could now see through the sloping glass roof of the conservatory to the interior. Two young men attired in striped blazers and white flannel trousers were sitting in wicker armchairs. Beside them, on a table, was a pair of straw boaters and two old-fashioned tennis rackets.

'They were very similar in looks. Both were tanned brown by the sun and had frank, open features. Their hair was dark, almost black, parted in the middle and shiny with brilliantine or some other oil. Their heads were half turned towards me as if, at any moment, they expected their partners to appear.

'I rapped on the pane and, to my consternation, one of the sisters appeared and, catching sight of me, gestured to me in the most emphatic manner to get down and go around to the front of the house. When I reached the door, it was already open. Both sisters were hopping about on the doorstep like agitated birds.

'Tall and slender with grey hair curling around the tops of their heads, they were wearing white voile tea dresses trimmed with lace. We went into the hall, past a stand in which there were walking sticks with carved wooden heads, faded parasols and a croquet mallet. I was ushered into a drawing room with gas wall lights and pink striped moiré paper.

'There were marble busts of famous explorers and watercolours of scenes of South America: a paddle steamer on the Amazon, a crumbling Mayan temple, a macaw in brilliant plumage. Aztec rugs were thrown over a sofa. The bookcases were crammed with books on tropical plants. The bluish-grey hide of a puma was stretched out on the floor.

'I picked my way among the clutter and sat at a round table next to Eleanor. Edith sat stiffly on a window seat. "Edith is very displeased with me for writing to you," said Eleanor. "We see very few people here and are rather out of sympathy with the world and its ways. I do not wish to seem discourteous but we are both a little tired and would like to make this visit a short one."

'I agreed with as much grace as I could muster. A tray laden with an elegant, bone-china tea set was produced and we made rather stilted conversation while I sipped at my cup and nibbled a cucumber sandwich.

Then Eleanor went to the piano and picked up a silver-gilt rose bowl.

'It was a fairly ordinary piece,' said Maggie, 'but I felt so guilty about the way I had behaved that I probably paid too much for it.'

'Very unlike you,' I teased. It was uncharitable but my mind was racing off in another direction.

She sighed and looked at her watch. 'I ought to get back to work.'

'And the conservatory? What did you make of what you saw?'

Maggie shook her head. 'I don't know what to make of it. It was rather like seeing a ghost – or rather, two ghosts. It upset me. I am trying to forget that it happened.'

I walked with Maggie back to her little van and returned to work but I found it impossible to concentrate. At lunchtime, I locked up the shop and went down the street to the church and sat in one of the pews at the back.

I closed my eyes and the images came flooding back. It was a few years earlier and December. I had been trading only for a few months and was just about breaking even. Then, in Christmas week, when we were all hoping to be doing good business, we had a heavy snowfall.

It was a Saturday and noon but there was not a buyer in sight and about a dozen of us locked up and trudged down to the church. We kicked the snow off our shoes and huddled around the brazier. The vicar provided some hot soup and mulled wine and we made a collection and put it in the offertory box.

Outside, the snow was falling steadily and no one wanted to go back to work.

Someone suggested that each of us told a story. After all, it was close to Christmas Eve. So, we made a circle of our chairs but then nobody wanted to begin and we drew lots. Percy drew the short straw – or matchstick, for that is what we used.

Percy Prettiman. That was his full name. His eyes were dark, almost black, and set in a thin face. His long nose and russet beard added to his foxy appearance. He had a green cloak which was threadbare and shiny with age. If someone told me that he lived in the woods and slept in it, I should not have been surprised.

Percy had a little shop next to mine from which he sold stuffed birds and animals in glass cases. These had long been out of fashion but he had a few 'regulars' which helped to keep him afloat. Nobody knew what age he was but he must have been close to seventy. He never stayed anywhere very long.

Percy sucked on an old briar, showing his yellow teeth, as he composed his thoughts. 'I am not much of a hand at stories, leastways not the sort that you make up in your head. I could tell you tales that I heard when I was a traveller, for I mixed with gypsies, vagrants, thieves, circus performers, defrocked priests, all sorts and conditions of men. But you might be more interested in something that happened to me a long time ago – nearly forty years by my reckoning.

'I was in an unusual line of business, one I learned from my father and he from his, and I journeyed all over the country selling patent medicines. I went on horseback and carried my equipment in two large saddlebags. Most of the houses that I visited belonged to the rich. In the years before The Great War, they led easy, comfortable lives with little to think about except their money, their social lives and their health.

'I did not always look the way I do now.' Percy ran a hand through his beard. 'On my horse, with my fresh complexion, my wide-brimmed hat and long cloak, there was many a girl who gave me a second glance. I was strong too. My arms were like steel bands and my skin as smooth as marble, for a man's form and features are shaped by the work that he does. In wrestling bouts at the summer fairs, I drew a good crowd and it was not just the men who wagered a shilling or two on me.

'One day, I was trotting along a track through the woods in the hills above Dorking. It was a very warm afternoon and I was glad of the shade from the trees. It was then that I thought I heard a cry. I dug my heels into my horse and galloped through the trees, praying that the brute would not put a hoof in a hole. Twice I thought I was lost but then I heard the cry again.

'I drew rein in front of a house in a small clearing in time to see two men being carried through the door. A young woman rushed up to me and seized the bridle of my horse. Despite her dishevelled hair and tear-stained face, she was one of the most beautiful creatures I have ever set eyes upon.

' *"Thank God!"* she cried. *"A doctor!"*

'I tried to explain that I was not a doctor although I had some experience of illness. She must call a proper doctor, I told her, but she would not listen.

'"There is no time," she sobbed. "Only you can save them." I threw the reins over a post and she clung to my arm and almost dragged me into the house.

'In the drawing room, I found the men laid out on two sofas. A fair-haired young lady, almost the twin in looks of the one who had greeted me, was being comforted by an old manservant.

'I examined both men. It did not take many moments to establish that both were beyond all human aid. The pupils of their eyes were enormously dilated and blisters were coming up on their faces, necks and hands. Soon they were running a high fever. Then delirium set in.

'Edith and Eleanor, for those were the names of the young women, were on their knees beside the men, holding their hands, crying out to them not to die, not to desert them. But it was useless. The poison was not just on their clothes, it had impregnated their skin. Within the hour they were in a deep coma from which they never emerged.

'After they had died, a remarkable change came over the two sisters. They drew down the blinds in the drawing room and we moved to the study. They were silent for some minutes and I can only guess what it cost them to compose themselves. At last, Edith wiped away a tear and drew a deep breath. "Mr Prettiman," she began, "you must be at a loss at what to think of the scene you have so recently witnessed. When I tell you something about Jerome and Neville and how my sister and I came to fall in love, you will know better how to help us.

'"My father was an eminent botanist who went to Brazil in search of rare plants with medicinal properties. He dreamed of finding a new species which would cure many different diseases but he was well aware that although they could be beneficial if absorbed into the body in tiny amounts, excessive exposure to them could be dangerous.

'"He sent seeds to this house to be propagated and nurtured by his gardener. His quest became an obsession and when his trips abroad turned into months, my mother insisted on joining him and brought Eleanor and myself.

'"One dreadful day, he walked into the jungle and did not return. Search parties were sent out but to no avail. Whether he had become lost and died or was killed by wild animals or some savage tribe was never discovered.

'"Our mother wasted no time on tears. She decided to go back to England and we set off in a paddle steamer bound for the nearest port for ocean-going vessels. One night, in a thick mist, the steamer collided with a dredger and was badly holed. She managed to save our lives but at the cost of her own.

'"We had no relatives in England. There was nothing to draw us there except this house which we inherited between us. We were educated and boarded at a mission school and did not return home until Eleanor was seventeen and I a year older.

'"On the liner, we met two brothers," said Edith. "I fell for Neville and Eleanor lost her heart to Jerome. It was no ordinary shipboard romance. Neville was three years older than I; the difference between Jerome's age and that of Eleanor was the same. We were soul mates from the first moment. We could not conceive of drawing a contented breath in the absence of the man we loved, let alone spending our days on this earth separated from him. We never discussed marriage.

There was no need for that. It was taken for granted that our lives would be joined together.

'"Jerome and Neville were returning to England for their last term at university. After taking their finals, they were to enjoy the summer holiday before returning to Brazil. Their parents owned a large ranch which had been in the family for several generations. They were getting old and infirm and were looking forward to handing over the reins to their sons."

'Edith showed signs of distress and after halting attempts to speak, she was unable to continue. Eleanor placed an arm around her sister and took up the story.

'"We had such fun during that last term. There were dances and tennis parties and trips down the river and when the summer holiday began, they hired a motor car and we drove across France to Monte Carlo. Edith and I chaperoned each other but only for form's sake. Our love ran so deep that we had no misgivings that they might try to take advantage of the trust that we placed in them."

'Eleanor stood up and moved to the window seat. The sun was lower in the sky and the glancing light turned her wheaten hair to gold. She compressed her lips and waited for a little nod from her sister before going on. "Jerome and Neville were very different in character."

'How different they were, she related, was not apparent until they returned to England to make plans for their passage to Brazil. Neville was already homesick for the ranching life. He wanted to bring Edith home to meet his parents and settle down and bring up a family.

'Jerome had been captivated by the glitter and sophistication of London and the south of France and he dreaded going back. He was willing to give his half of his inheritance to his brother. He would marry Eleanor, remain in England and build up a business importing foodstuffs and herbs from the Americas.

'As for Edith, she could not bear the thought of being separated from Eleanor by thousands of miles of ocean but if they all moved to South America, she despaired of what would happen to Aruana and their father's work, for which he gave his life.'

Percy drained his glass and, pulling a handkerchief from his sleeve, wiped his lips. 'Earlier, on that last afternoon, Jerome and Neville took a train to the nearest station to Aruana. The sisters met them in the pony and trap. The young men accompanied them back to the house where they confirmed that they had booked their passages to São Paulo on a steamer which sailed from Southampton the next day.

'But nothing had been resolved. The brothers argued. Accusation and counter-accusation flew across the room. When the quarrel became heated, they went into the garden. Edith and Eleanor heard raised voices but thought it best not to interfere and they left the men alone.

'You can imagine their horror when the gardener came running up to the door to say that he had heard the sound of panes in the greenhouse being smashed and found the men fighting on the floor. The sisters ran to the greenhouse but the poison had already done its work. In the struggle, both had suffered cuts from falling glass. Some of the tropical plants had been knocked over, crushing the leaves, and the sap had got into their wounds.'

Percy looked around his audience and gave a little shrug. 'There is not much more to tell. The sisters asked me whether I thought that they could get special permission for Jerome and Neville to be buried at Aruana. In that way, they would always be together. But even if that was allowed, would the brothers' parents ever sanction it?

'That seemed so improbable that I could not, in good faith, offer a word of encouragement. Then, in an extraordinary twist of fate, the steamer on which they had booked their passage was caught in a terrible storm in the Bay of Biscay and was lost. There were no survivors. The reservations for Jerome and Neville had not been cancelled. Perhaps the records of the shipping company were not all that they should have been. In any event, the brothers' parents received a cable informing them, with great regret, that their sons had gone down with the vessel.'

Percy put a match to the bowl of his old briar and then, remembering where he was, put it out. 'I would have done anything for those two girls,' he muttered. 'Anything at all.'

Someone asked him the question to which we all wanted an answer but he was busy stamping his feet on the stone floor and may not have heard it. Then he looked up at the window and announced that it had stopped snowing and we should all go back to work.

A few weeks later, without any warning, Percy was gone. A policeman called and made rather desultory enquiries after him. I inquired whether he was in any sort of trouble. Mr Prettiman's father and grandfather ran a firm of undertakers, he told me.

'Their speciality was what is known in the profession as 'restorative services'. The firm was undercapitalised and eventually went bankrupt. Young Percy took to the road selling his patent medicines. But a trade once learned cannot be unlearned.'

'Bereavement is a painful business, Officer.'

'So it is. People want to help and sometimes sympathy or money persuades them to do more than they should.' There had been rumours, he told me, of 'irregularities'.

Orange Hat

The morning post clattered into the letter box. Ralph left his chair, collected the envelopes and opened them. The effect these letters made could hardly have been more remarkable. For the next half an hour accusations, protestations and recriminations blazed back and forth across the breakfast table. The bank statement lay between them, a reproachful red stain against the white tablecloth, and near it a small pile of unpaid bills. Anna's makeshift defences had blown away in the storm. She was almost in tears. Ralph softened a little.

'I have told you again and again, my darling,' he said, 'we cannot afford the money you are spending. Martin will soon be going to day school and there is this house to pay for. We have got to watch every penny. This extravagance must stop and must stop now.'

'Brute,' Anna muttered. 'All this fuss over a few measly hats.'

Ralph's heavy eyebrows contracted. 'Hats are your vice and you know it,' he said. 'Your father warned me the day I married you. "Watch out for Anna's hat-trick," he told me, "or she will ruin you." Heaven knows what your hats have cost us these last four years. There are hats bulging from every cupboard and drawer. Pink hats, blue hats, silk and straw hats, large and small hats, fur hats. Sometimes I think that this house is nothing more than a huge hatbox.'

Anna was silent. How pretty she looks, he thought, her blue eyes downcast, her face with a high colour sheltering among an abundance of corn-coloured hair.

Ralph turned once more to the bills for the strength he needed. 'This must be the last of these bills,' he went on. 'I see that Mrs Thankerton's is the worst as usual. Now you must promise to keep away from that shop, and the others, until you have learnt to control yourself.' For good measure, he added, 'And you had better stay clear of the Drews. Rosemary Drew is almost as bad as you are. You two egg each other on. How that fool Brian can afford to indulge her, I don't know.'

It was true. Ever since they had left school together, Rosemary and Anna had vied with each other in their choice of clothes. In this battle, hats, it was mutually conceded, were the most potent weapons. Shortly after Anna's marriage, Rosemary had married Brian Drew. Brian had courted Anna quite seriously at one time and the two were still close friends. The fierce but friendly rivalry between the girls continued much as before. It simply became sharper and more expensive.

'Rosemary knows nothing about hats,' said Anna.

Ralph stood up. With a sweep of his arm he gathered hat, umbrella and the morning paper. His other arm went round Anna and he kissed her. 'So you are going to reform, my sweet. Promise?'

Anna nodded dismally.

'No lapses,' he went on, 'no last chances, no excuses. I'm serious.'

Anna shook her head.

'You know I don't like the role of the heavy-handed husband, but I will play it if I have to.'

She nodded again.

'Well, that's settled,' he concluded. 'Now, I shall be late.'

Ralph went away up the front path and off to work. He was beyond the garden gate before Anna could summon the rebel strength and courage to shout after him. 'What happened to the romantic I thought I married?' she cried. 'He's just a solid earth-bound Englishman after all.' She added a last taunt, 'I'll have your slippers and pipe ready for you when you come home this evening.'

Ralph turned and waved. Anna could not be sure that he had heard. She blew her nose and shut the door.

The housework normally took a couple of hours at the most. Anna devoted the whole morning to it. Self-discipline, she said to herself, that was the answer to her problem. Things that didn't need doing she did once, tasks that did, she performed twice. By lunchtime she loved Ralph again. The stand he had taken had seemed petty and unfair but she could see now that he had been justice and moderation itself. How thoughtless and selfish she had been, how childish this rivalry with Rosemary now seemed.

She would make amends. That afternoon, she resolved, would be given over to Martin, their small son. She would take him to the park. Jacko, their dog, could come too. She would keep far away from her favourite shops. Yet, this still did not seem enough. Somehow, Anna felt, she must purge, eradicate once and for all this weakness of hers. An idea struck her. She possessed one hat, a single disastrous failure, a hideous orange affair with tassels, shaped like an upturned flowerpot.

It had been worn but once and had narrowly escaped being burnt. She had kept it as a warning to herself that even the most discerning are capable of unaccountable lapses of taste. At whatever cost to her pride, Anna resolved, she would wear that hat for her walk. It would be an act of expiation for her past folly. Ralph would return that evening to a responsible and contrite woman.

It was a wonderful autumn afternoon. Anna sighed. She would have paid homage to such a day. A visit to Mrs Thankerton's shop and a lovely new hat would have been a fitting tribute. But it must not be. She went to the wardrobe. Dozens of hats, glamorous competitors, seemed to press forward as she opened the door.

Grimly ignoring their claims, she plucked the shameful orange object from its hiding place at the back and rammed it on her head. Six monstrous hatpins set the seal on her disgrace. Heaven preserve me from recognition, she prayed. Martin, and his pram were collected. Jacko, the fat and disobedient cocker spaniel, was persuaded to leave his basket and accompany them. Together they set out.

To avoid passing near the enticing shops, she made a wide detour. Her hat provoked curious smiles but she affected to ignore them. At last, thankfully, she steered the pram into the park. She brightened. It was hard to be gloomy on such a glorious day. Jacko was let off his lead and scampered on ahead as fast as his stout body would allow him. Martin was a delight. Horses, poodles, pigeons and ducks, he had to admire each in turn.

Afterwards they sat together by the pond for hours in the sunshine. Every model boat that pulled in to shore had to pass Martin's rigorous inspection before being allowed to continue its voyage. By the time the last trim white yacht had been sent scudding across the water back to its anxious owner, pursued by the boy's ecstatic applause, the sun was low in the evening sky.

Anna looked at her watch; she could turn for home and safety. Martin had to have his bath and supper and there was dinner to get ready, then Ralph would be back. She put her son back in the pram. Jacko, barking, started off ahead again as they moved off. Anna found herself looking forward to Ralph's return with that heightened sense of pleasure that only a clear conscience affords.

She reached the edge of the park. She would go home, she had decided, following the same circuitous route that she had taken earlier in the afternoon. But Jacko had different ideas. He galloped straight on. Nothing was going to stop him going back his usual way. There was a pet shop that way and a kind lady behind the counter. Jacko always went in on the way past and the kind lady never failed to reward him with something nice to eat.

Ignoring Anna's shouts and whistles and contemptuous of the speeding cars and buses, Jacko scurried across the road. Anna cursed her luck. To follow him would take her where of all places she wished to avoid. But there was no alternative. She must catch the dog. With growing apprehension she set off after him.

People were hurrying back from work. Avoiding them was a task in itself. Anna absorbed herself in the chase, guiding the pram swiftly along the pavements. Puff and strain as he might, the fat Jacko was no match for her but it took Anna two streets or more to catch him. He was scolded and put on his lead.

She rested for a moment and looked about her. It was as bad, or worse, than she had feared. She was in the heart of her forbidden paradise. She had travelled so far, it was as dangerous to go back as to go on. But if she must run the gauntlet of these shops, her best hope, she decided, lay in speed.

Anna stepped out. The shops seemed to lie in wait for her. Treasure houses bursting out as she passed in an ambush of coats and gowns and dresses of every colour and description. There were hats too. Gathered there were the most daring and astonishing, the most fascinating, the most outrageous, the vainest, the silliest, the prettiest, the most desirable hats imaginable.

Anna was almost running now, careless of the stares she received. As the pram bore down on them, startled pedestrians leaped aside. Martin, jumping up and down in his speeding chariot in a frenzy of excitement, bellowed encouragement to the exhausted and disconsolate Jacko who trailed like an anchor behind.

Suddenly Anna hauled the pram to a halt. She stared up the street, a look of agonised suspicion on her face. Barely two hundred yards away, a very smartly dressed couple were standing looking into a shop window. As they turned towards her, Anna found that terrible suspicion confirmed.

Unmistakably the pair was Brian and Rosemary Drew. Rosemary, she could now see, looked superb; Brian, magnificent. It was a waking nightmare. Frozen into near paralysis by the sight, crowned in her appalling, almost blasphemous headgear, Anna stood and stared.

Slowly, painfully, her brain accepted the evidence of her eyes but her returning faculties impressed upon her the significance of what, instinctively, she already knew. If Rosemary saw her in this hat, it meant not only the end of her precarious ascendancy over her rival, not just defeat, but annihilation. As for Brian, she valued his admiration more than she would have cared to admit. It would be the end. She could not envisage life after it.

Yet, it was just possible that she might escape detection. Hope gave Anna a desperate energy. She pulled the pram sharply into a doorway. But what if they saw her there? There was no cover and they must be upon her at any moment.

Panic possessed her. How could she get rid of this hat! She fumbled at hatpins, pulled, tugged, tore at the hat itself. Uselessly. It sat, stubbornly clamped to her head.

A neat, elderly grey-haired woman appeared from a door. 'Perhaps I can help,' she said, smiling.

'*Mrs Thankerton!*' she gasped. She could have screamed, though whether with mortification or relief she did not know. 'Rosemary Drew nearly had me cornered that tine,' she cried. *'She's dressed to kill!'*

Mrs Thankerton struggled with her curiosity. 'Yes,' she replied, 'Mrs Drew must be on her way here now. She has an appointment just before six.'

'*What! Rosemary's coming here!*' Anna felt on the point of collapse. '*Quickly! Mrs Thankerton!*' she implored. 'Please help me out of this ghastly hat and–' she had caught sight of the wonderful display inside the shop, 'do let me try on that gorgeous blue bonnet, the one with the long feathers.'

It was the work of a few seconds. Anna was transfigured, transported even. She was in her heaven. At that moment, Martin in his pram, Jacko, the Drews, all belonged to another world. Slowly she pirouetted before the glass. *'Exquisite!'* she pronounced at last.

Rosemary and Brian came in. Brian gave Anna a marvellous smile. From Rosemary, she won a look of grudging approval. Anna sighed gratefully. 'I think I'll take this hat, Mrs Thankerton,' she said.

'Robber!' exclaimed Rosemary. 'You have stolen the blue bonnet. I had my eye on that beauty. Never mind,' she went on, 'Mrs Thankerton and I, between us, will find something nicer even if it takes all night. Brian,' she added, 'I'll be here for ages. You will be so bored. Why don't you walk Anna home?'

Anna protested feebly but she and Brian pushed the pram away together. 'Behave yourselves,' Rosemary called after them mischievously. Jacko strained at his lead, impatient to be back.

Ralph opened the door when they arrived. He looked at the bonnet and he looked at Anna.

'Behold your wife!' Brian cried. He never felt quite at ease with Ralph. 'Sporting a new headdress in your honour!' He struck an attitude familiar to those introducing fashion displays, 'A magnificent creation from the emporium of the inimitable Mrs Thankerton!'

Anna felt rather faint. 'You ... you are back early, Ralph,' she stammered. It was all she could think of.

Ralph said very little. Brian thought he seemed rather short. He waved goodbye. They went inside and closed the door.

Anna took Martin up to bath. Ralph said nothing, not even 'pompous ass,' his usual comment on Brian. It was disconcerting. Anna felt vaguely menaced. With every moment of unbroken silence, the atmosphere seemed to grow more oppressive. By the time she reached the top of the first flight, it was almost more than she could bear.

Then Ralph spoke. Anna stopped and stayed there, motionless. *'Anna!'* he said. 'Do you remember the slippers and pipe you were talking about this morning? Well, I should like just one slipper. One should be enough. Bring it down, please, when you have finished with Martin.'

It wasn't a question. It was an order. Anna remained silent. The heavy-handed husband, she thought. Well, anything, even that, would be easier than trying to explain. Clutching her new hat tightly, she went on up the stairs.

Footsteps

Julian Stanford sharpened his pencil for the third time that morning before starting on the other end. He looked at his cheap wristwatch and then craned his neck in an effort to make out the position of the hands on Liz Makin's Rolex. If he took the average between the two readings, converted it to a decimal, multiplied it by the number of flies on the ceiling and divided it by the loose change in his pocket, he could probably waste at least ten minutes – anything to provide a distraction from leafing through the dreary piles of estate agents' particulars in front of him. But no, a malign fate appeared to have synchronised the timepieces. With a deep sigh he turned his head to the window beside his desk, squinting between the rows of perspex frames with their property advertisements like a prisoner peering between the bars of his cell for a glimpse of the world outside.

'If you can't keep your mind on your job, Stanford, I can see we shall have to move your desk into the corner,' Mr Sprague boomed at him from the doorway of his office. 'This is your second week with us and I hope we are going to get more work out of you than we did in your first. We have two negotiators on holiday so there's no shortage of work. And remember, Stanford, you are on a month's probation. We don't carry passengers in this firm.'

'Yes, Mr Sprague – I mean no, Mr Sprague.' Julian pushed his calculator back in the drawer and took out an old grey rubber. Mr Sprague hovered for a moment like a dark thundercloud and then stumped back to his desk. Julian worked away at his rubber until he had sketched a tolerable likeness of Mr Sprague's face and then, adding a vicious point to his pencil, drove it into the manager's scowling mouth. He skewered it round and round, excavating little tooth-like shards and then withdrew his harpoon. Mr Sprague howled in agony.

Liz Makin put down the telephone and walked briskly across the office to a board on the wall festooned with keys hanging from little brass hooks. As she stretched up, her navy-blue skirt rode up the neat curves of her rump revealing the hem of a white satin slip and affording a tantalising glimmer of white thighs above sheer silk stocking tops. She swivelled on her high heels and caught his eyes on her. Her chin went up an insolent notch. 'I have got a viewing in Park Mansions, Julian. I'll be about thirty minutes. Try not to cause too much chaos while I'm out.' He glowered at her, making a token swipe at the door handle as she came past him but she was there first and he watched her stride away, her dark hair scything away from her head like the knives on Boadicea's chariot.

Julian let out a deep sigh. He had been born twenty years too late, missed out on that golden age when girls like Liz sat drooping in their wretched bedsitters every evening waiting for the telephone to ring. Now they had careers, bought their own flats, paid for their own dinners and drove sports cars. Judging by the magazines they read, they enjoyed frenetic sex lives. He never seemed to meet any girls. But what could you expect if you lived in a flat in your parents' house? And if you had parents like his?

His mother was a tall, spare woman with long, untidy limbs and the awkward movements of a crane fly. Her sole interest in life was the wilderness between the back of the house and the railway line where she grew the wild flowers and herbs that went into the rows of miniature bottles in the larder cupboard where she stored her remedies. That and the small band of disciples who come to the house on Tuesday afternoons to sip rose-hip tea and listen to a talk from an invited speaker on 'The natural world of healing'.

His father, Harold, was a stipendiary magistrate in one of the London courts and an authoritarian of the old school. 'It's long past time that you decided what you are going to do with your life, my boy. You won't find the answer lying on that sofa all day watching the television.' His strictures, bellowed down the stairs to the flat in the basement, became as regular and predictable as the catchphrases in the beer advertisements.

Eventually his father had lost patience. 'You had better go into the law since you have no ideas of your own. Your Uncle William has agreed to give you a fortnight's work experience at the end of term. He took some persuading, I don't mind telling you. Solicitors' firms are not a soft touch these days. They can pick and choose.'

'Yes, Father.'

'If he likes the look of you, he will put you on his list for articles. But the rest is up to you. You will have to work like hell to get to university and then get your grades. So don't let me down.'

For the only two weeks of the summer holidays when it stopped raining and the sun shone gloriously, he had trailed across London to the dismal alleyway off the Gray's Inn Road where Harben, Beasley and Rhodes conducted their business.

He was given a desk in a gloomy office with a narrow window looking out on a light well, if a small yard bounded by blackened brickwork and rusty downpipes, littered with pigeon droppings and smelling faintly of drains can be so described, and for his sole companion, a sallow-faced, taciturn young man with a disconcerting twitch.

Long periods of indolence were punctuated with brief flurries of photocopying, filing and tea-making. His uncle had visited him but once, interrupting his examination of the mummified carcase of a tiger moth which he had discovered pressed between the mildewed leaves of *Knecker on Probate and Trusts*.

His father summoned him to his study. 'Your uncle wasn't very encouraging.'

'No, Father.'

'We will talk about it again when we get your exam results.'

'Yes, Father.'

Unfortunately for his father's ambitions, his examination results had been execrable and hopes of getting to university were abandoned. He had been rather looking forward to three years of leisurely introspection with a barricade of cloisters and quadrangles, quirky pipe-smoking dons and burly college porters between him and the world outside.

'It's a pity,' his mother said. 'It would have been a chance for the boy to find himself.'

A succession of job interviews made it clear that this was a quest that prospective employers were unlikely to support. 'You will just have to learn to stand on your own feet,' his father said. 'Go down to the Jobcentre and take what's on offer. Get some experience under your belt. There's no school like the school of life.'

'A bit of a sportsman, are we?' the clerk behind the window had inquired, casting a speculative eye over Julian's tweed jacket and corduroy trousers. 'The Dalston Animal Sanctuary is looking for someone to join their Recovery Team – rounding up stray dogs and that – but you'll need a doctor's certificate to show that you've had your jabs.'

'*Jabs!*' He was startled.

'Inoculations. One of their blokes got bitten last week. Went down with lockjaw – swallowed his tongue.'

Julian gulped. 'Have you ... something a little less...'

'Less exciting?' The clerk sucked the end of his pencil, 'There's a hospital porter's job going. What about that?'

He had taken it. The hospital was a rambling Victorian building and this, indirectly, led to a misadventure. He had only been there a few weeks when he lost himself in the maze of featureless corridors while wheeling an elderly, feeble-minded patient from her ward to the physiotherapy department.

After twenty minutes of fruitless peregrination, his charge, a diminutive, white-haired old lady became fractious and, thrashing the air with her stick, insisted that he should leave her and go in search of help. He pushed the wheelchair into a small, windowless room and left her, appeased for the moment, gazing with rapt attention at an enigmatic circular aperture in the ceiling immediately above her head.

He eventually tracked down a helpful orderly who took him to a large wall chart and patiently explained the layout of the hospital. 'You must be somewhere near the laundry room,' the man suggested. 'All the sheets and towels come down from the upper floors.' There was a reverberation like distant thunder and a slight tremor ran through the building. The orderly cocked his head, 'There! What did I tell you? That's the chute you can hear now.'

For a month he had sat in his tiny sitting room addressing envelopes. It was work for which he still had to be paid. Every morning he telephoned to ask about his money. The message was always the same. A cheque was in the post. One morning he rang and received no reply. The telephone had been cut off.

Morale had suffered. Life seemed quite pointless. It was difficult to find a sensible reason for getting up at all. He had lain in bed listening to his father hammering on the breakfast table.

'*Phyllis!* Can't you get that son of yours up in the morning?'

There were a few winged days as a motorcycle courier culminating in a desperate wobble one dark, wet evening which had deposited a package of expensive artwork under the wheels of a double-decker bus. His mother made up a tincture of yellow jasmine and gave it to him in a little warm cooking brandy. 'It will settle your nerves, dear.'

He took almost a week to recover, lying prostrate on the sofa in the darkened room listening to his Bruce Springsteen tapes and philosophising upon the meaning of life. The human race, he decided, was like the enormous jigsaw puzzle that his uncle produced for their annual visit on Boxing Day. There were the easy pieces which fitted readily but there were others so recalcitrant that they were still scattered around the edge of the table when it was time to abandon the project and go home. He emerged from his purdah in a mood of cheerful resignation.

His father was ready for him. 'I will be in my study,' he barked as he rose from the table. 'I can give you five minutes. *Now!*'

When his father was angry, his face turned a dusky red and the tufts in his ears seemed to bristle, giving him the appearance of an infuriated gooseberry. He stood with his back to the fireplace tugging fiercely at a cigarette. 'I've got you a month's trial with Fulford Fallow. Estate agents. Chelsea branch. I had to go cap in hand to John Fallow. I hardly know the man. And I had to give him lunch.'

'What do I–'

'Let me finish. There's not much money, a low basic salary plus commission – use of a company car. Showing people around flats.' He threw his cigarette, half smoked, into the grate.

'You are up to that I suppose?' His son supposed that he was.

'Well, get yourself tidied up. Here's a tenner for a haircut.' He took a note from his pocketbook. 'Your mother has pressed your suit. Get your shoes polished. This is probably your last chance to make something of yourself. So don't let me down.'

***

Julian watched a pigeon strutting along the railing outside. Up and down, up and down. He opened a drawer to consult his journal and turned to the page headed Pigeons. It was where he kept a tally of the number of patrols completed before the inevitable squirt of white graffiti on the shiny black paintwork and the bird flew off. He made a note in the book. Perhaps this was how Darwin got started.

'It's time we let that apartment in Admirals Court,' Mr Sprague called out from his office.

'Yes, Mr Sprague.' He could see the manager's feet under his desk pedalling up and down, up and down. He hadn't the energy to add this new phenomenon to his observations. Wearily he dug into the pile of brochures and retrieved the details. *Magnificently appointed ninth floor apartment,* he read. *Probably the finest property currently available on the London market ... fully furnished ... superb balcony views ... prestigious waterside setting ... unrivalled facilities ... fitness club ... tennis court ... heated indoor swimming pool.* He sighed. What wouldn't he give to live in a place like that? He could see it all. Dinner on the balcony under the stars, a beautiful woman across the table, candlelight, champagne, soft music coming from somewhere...

'I had Victor Skordias on the telephone after you had gone home yesterday.'

'The Greek ship owner, Mr Sprague?'

'Correct. He and his wife are over here for ten days. Some big business conference. They own the penthouse flat on the tenth floor. They must be worth millions.'

But Julian had lost interest. He turned over the brochure. At the bottom of the page there was a layout plan. Idly he sketched a pair of feet walking from the lift lobby to the front door of the apartment.

A pale shadow fell across his desk. Someone was looking at the properties advertised in the window. The door opened and he busied himself with his papers, conscious only that a woman had come in and was standing in front of his desk. 'I wonder if you can help me,' she said. 'I am looking for somewhere to live. Somewhere rather special.'

He didn't look up at once, intrigued by her voice, trying to match the husky undertones to the long red brocaded coat, the black sable cuffs and hem. She removed her fur hat and shook out her hair. It was as if she had released a cloud of goldfinches.

He stood open-mouthed looking at her. For the life of him he could not have uttered. He had walked into the sea and been caught by a huge breaker which had knocked all the breath from his body.

She smiled at him. 'It would be wonderful to have somewhere near the river. I think water is so romantic, don't you?'

The perfume that she was wearing was light and subtle. A hint of lily of the valley, of a woodland in spring ... clear pools ... he looked into her eyes ... and bluebells ... bluebells as far as you could see.

'Blue...' he said in a small, strangled voice.

She laughed, a tinkling sound like ice melting in pale, early morning sunshine, and borne away on the stream. 'I won't make you promise that my river will always be blue, but please do your best.'

Mr Sprague had been making low growling sounds in his office like a dog chained in a backyard. Now he came to the door. 'Perhaps I can be of assistance, Madam?' His trousers had bagged at the knees. He ran his hands down his thighs in a fruitless attempt to iron out the creases.

The young woman turned to him, 'How very kind of you, but please do not trouble yourself. Your colleague is attending to me.'

Mr Sprague pursed his lips and with a scowl at Julian, clumped back to his desk.

She rounded her eyes at the departing figure, pressing her teeth into her upper lip like a mischievous schoolgirl baiting teacher. 'My name is Suki Renouf.'

'Julian Stanford.'

She pressed his hand lightly, 'I shall call you Mr Standfast. You shall be my tower of strength.'

'I shall try to be.' He fetched her a chair and with a little sigh she sat down. She had been travelling around the world for several years, she told him. 'I have been everywhere and seen everything. I'm tired of it, Mr Standfast. I want to make my home here. I want to put down some roots.'

'Are you ... by yourself?' he inquired timidly. How was it possible that such a creature had not already been ensnared by some collector of exotica and locked away with his other trophies?

'Oh, quite alone.' The corners of her mouth drooped for a moment. Then her eyes lit up like a child invited to a party. 'But everything is going to be different from now on, isn't that right, Mr Standfast?' She picked up the brochure and crossed her hands over it, holding it to her heart. 'I have a feeling about this place and I'm never wrong about my feelings.'

'Admirals Court is very expensive,' he began, 'there are cheaper apartments.' A rumbling sound came from the manager's office.

She giggled. 'Dear Mr Standfast, I can see that you are determined to look after me. But don't worry too much.' She lowered her voice, 'You will think me dreadfully spoiled but money isn't a problem. I can pay six months in advance. Or a year if you prefer.'

'If you think that you would be happy there–'

'That is all that matters. To be happy. When I open my eyes each morning,' she fluttered her long lashes into wakefulness, 'I want to feel as if I am on holiday, as if all the people I most want to see are on their way to call on me.' She twirled her hat on the end of her finger. 'Life should be one long carnival. Don't you agree, Mr Standfast?'

He nodded mournfully. If only it were. But he and Suki lived on different planets. He could never share even the smallest corner of her life. The sunlight that warmed her by day, the moon that slept upon her pillow at night were closer to her than he could ever hope to be.

Suki leafed through the pages of the brochure. She seemed to pause for a moment over the layout plan and he felt his face reddening as he remembered his infantile doodling.

'Forgive me,' he muttered. 'I will find a clean copy for you.' He hurried across the room to the filing cabinet. Mr Sprague appeared at his shoulder, hanging over him like a vast spoil heap.

'*What has got into you today, Stanford?*' he hissed. 'Ask Miss Renouf whether she would like to view the apartment. She can be driven there at once. Explain that we have keys and would be pleased to accompany her.'

'Yes, Mr Sprague.' He almost choked on the words. Tears of rage and humiliation pricked at his eyes. To be scolded in front of Suki! To be treated like the merest clerk! But she was shaking her head, she wouldn't do what Mr Sprague wanted. He could have thrown his arms about her and kissed her!

'No, thank you ever so much. I will just take the details if I may. I am meeting some friends at Claridges for lunch and I am rather pressed for time. I have a car waiting. So, if you don't mind, I will be on my way.'

Mr Sprague returned to his office, shutting the door sharply behind him. Suki took the brochure with a smile of sympathy.

'You will come back when you have read it?' he entreated. He couldn't bear to see her go. When she left she would leave him in darkness like an eclipse of the sun.

Suki moved a little nearer and put a hand on his arm. Her closeness made him feel dizzy. 'I promise,' she said softly.

He held the door for her, his eyes following her as she tripped across the pavement to where a uniformed chauffeur stood waiting beside a shiny black saloon. A gloved hand waved at him. Then she was gone.

He went back to his desk, his back bent like a galley slave granted an hour of freedom and now returning to the thwarts to serve out his sentence.

The door of the back office opened and Mr Sprague reappeared. 'Congratulations, Stanford! The first good prospect that we have had in weeks and you let her get away.'

'But Mr Sprague,' he protested, 'she will be back.'

'Maybe. Maybe not. I wouldn't count on it. Do you know where she is staying?'

Julian hung his head and made no answer.

The manager smiled sardonically. 'Then I think you have lost her. People like that don't walk in every day, you know.'

Julian wanted to scream at him, *'No! But people like you do!'*

Mr Sprague consulted his watch. 'It's time for my lunch.' He patted his paunch complacently. As he came to Julian's desk he paused and seemed to take satisfaction in his colleague's crestfallen expression. 'You have got to learn to take the knocks in this business, Stanford.' He sucked his teeth noisily. 'When you have been around as long as I have you'll find that out.' He opened the door and went out, whistling tunelessly.

Julian slumped over his desk, resting his cheek on the corner of the brochure that Suki had held between her fingers. If she didn't come back, he would sink into melancholy and just pine away.

There was a rattle of the door and Liz swept into the room. 'Keeping busy, I see,' she said. She went to her message pad and then to the keyboard. 'I have got a viewing in Castlerosse House. I'll be about an hour.'

'We have got some interest in Admirals–' he began, but she was already out of earshot and he watched her swinging her legs expertly into her BMW. She revved the engine and zipped out into the traffic.

His eyes fell to the heap of leaflets in front of him. Houses and flats, maisonettes and duplexes, freeholds and leaseholds, long leases, short leases, to rent and to buy. The detritus of other people's lives. Lives that were meaningless to him. For all the interest he could summon up, their dwellings might be so many defunct molehills.

He cleared a space on his desk and opened up the brochure on Admirals Court, debating with himself how many forms of construction the publication might lend itself to ... a tent ... an open hanger ... he stared at it, feeling his hair rising at the nape of his neck, the skin on his upper arms prickling like nettle rash.

On the layout plan where he had placed his line of footprints, another set of prints had been added. The lonely track of prints had found their twin. Not one but two people now left the lift together and walked across the lobby to the apartment. But that was not all. He bent over the diagram, his heart racing. The new line of footsteps did not stop, as did his, at the front door. They crossed the hall and advanced along the passage until they reached the entrance to the reception room. In a fever of excitement, he took his pen and extended his line of prints until the two phantoms stood side by side.

The next day there was no sign of her. Nor the following day. The plan on the brochure tormented him. A hundred times he told himself that it meant nothing, that Suki had no interest in him, that what she had done was no more than the whim of an idle moment. But he longed to believe that she had spun this long thread, placed one end of it in his hands.

Then, on the third day, shortly before two o'clock, he saw her car draw up outside. The chauffeur ran around to open her door and she stepped out. She was wearing a blue blazer with golden buttons down the front. The matching skirt was cut daringly high. An expensive bag in dark-blue leather swung from her shoulder. She was hatless and the light breeze toyed with her hair. It was like the sun coming out from behind a cloud.

'All the others are out,' he told her exultantly, waving at the empty desks.

'And the ogre in the cave?' she rolled her eyes in the direction of the rear office.

He laughed with her. 'Mr Sprague's at lunch. Every day he leaves at exactly a quarter to one and goes to the Rat and Carrot down the road for his steak and kidney pudding and a pint of bitter. The routine never varies. He has been doing that for over twenty years.'

'Oh dear!' She settled her long fair hair on her shoulders and surveyed his gloomy prison. 'It must be so difficult for someone so young and vital and ...' she pressed her lips together as if unsure how to continue, 'and attractive ... to be shut up in this place.'

He turned away quickly. Never in his life had anyone said such a thing to him. He wanted to go somewhere quiet, where he could be alone and repeat those words to himself, over and over again.

It was as if she had read his mind. 'I mustn't keep you,' she said. 'I have got such a lot of shopping to do.'

He fingered the brochure. 'Would you like to see–'

'No, not just yet.' She opened the clasp of her shoulder bag. 'Please let me have details on some of the other properties you are handling.' Her eyes went to the filing cabinet. 'I don't think one should rush at these things. Don't you agree, Mr Standfast?'

'Oh, I do so very much agree.' Their eyes met for a split second and then, like an actor late on cue, he hurried over to the cabinet. His fingers were trembling and he scrabbled around in the files, hardly able to see for the perspiration in his eyes. He had to force himself not to turn his head to watch her for fear of severing this tenuous link that bound them.

Suki tucked away the brochures, gave his hand a little squeeze and left. He watched her chauffeur give a final polish to the already gleaming bodywork before the car pulled away from the kerb and disappeared up the road.

Some movement caught his eye. Mr Sprague was on his way back. It was like a cloud passing over the sun. Even that small exertion seemed too much, for when he arrived he was out of breath. 'Any calls for me?' he panted.

'No, Mr Sprague, nothing,' he replied distractedly. He wanted to look at the plan on the brochure. Had Suki extended her footsteps down the passage? It was torture not knowing. If only the man would go back to his room.

The manager took a not over-clean handkerchief from his pocket and wiped his forehead. 'I hope that Renouf woman of yours isn't a time-waster,' he grumbled.

'Oh, I'm sure she is not,' Stanford exclaimed. 'You have only to look at her clothes and her car. She is obviously very well off.'

Mr Sprague sniffed. A small flake of pastry was sticking to the corner of his mouth. Julian watched it, fascinated to see whether it would fall off when he started to speak. 'When you have been in this game as long as I have, you won't be sure of anything.' He eased his trouser band over his belly and stumped off to the lavatory.

It took Julian a few nerve-wracking moments to find the brochure, which had been hidden under his blotting pad. His mouth was dry and there was a band around his chest which hurt him when he breathed. He took a lightning glance at it like a camera on a split-second exposure and pushed it away from him. He stood up, passing a hand over his forehead. It was cold and damp with perspiration. He wondered if he was going to faint.

Liz ran through the door, retrieved a sandwich out of a drawer, took two bites and jingled a set of keys at him, *'Got to fly!'* she said, through a mouthful of cream cheese. 'That old witch Lady Dibden wants to go round Dove Place. *For the third time!'*

'How long will you be?' His voice came out as a hoarse croak.

'Not long.' She looked at him curiously. 'Go and get some lunch. You look like death warmed up.' She peeped into the back office. 'Where's Sprague?'

'In the loo. He was trying to hide the *Evening Standard* under his jacket.'

'Then he will be in there for ages.' She wrinkled her nose. The door closed behind her.

He sat down again, loosened his tie, undid the top button of his shirt and closed his eyes. Suki was moving too fast for him. Things were getting out of control. Her latest prints had left him standing by the entrance to the reception room, while hers had walked up the passage and gone into the kitchen. But they hadn't stayed there. They emerged and continued until they reached the dining room. At that point the shape of the prints changed. The length of stride shortened, the heel and instep disappeared leaving only the ball of the foot and the toe. It was as if she was moving on tiptoe. The prints came to a standstill at the door to the master bedroom.

His heart was jumping like a March hare. Had Suki fallen for him? Sent him a coded message that she wanted to have an affair with him? Nothing else made sense. Was Admirals Court to be a place of assignation? He wrapped his arms about him, hugging himself. If Amanda and Kate could see him now, wouldn't they kick themselves? They had their chances at the Christmas party and what did they do? Pulled faces when he asked them to dance, made absurd excuses about being tired or having to go home early. And then he had found them downstairs smooching in the disco with Hugo and Ian. He had been cast down for weeks.

He went to Liz's desk and pulled open the top drawer. There at the back he found the small hand mirror that she used to repair her make-up. He puffed at the glass and gave it a rub with his sleeve. Young, vital and attractive. Those were Suki's very words. His reflection stared back at him gloomily as if reproaching him for having given it so little fun in all the years that they had been together. He wondered what it would feel like to have Suki's long, elegant fingers running through his hair, gliding over the soft waves, playing with the roguish lock which fell over an ear, caressing it into place.

He grinned into the mirror. He wished he owned a smile like an American film star, a smile as wide as a slice of watermelon. His mouth was too small. Mean.

Niggardly. He pushed his fingers between his lips and tugged at the corners but it hurt too much to continue. Film stars probably wore a metal plate at night which stretched their mouths like those savages whose photographs he had seen in geographical magazines with their grotesquely protruding lips.

As for his chin, he couldn't boast a cleft like Michael Douglas or Cary Grant but he possessed a small dimple. Perhaps, in time, it would develop into a feature that would knock the girls sideways. And his eyes. How could the hateful Amanda say that they were muddy, the taunt that she had flung at him when he had reproached her for some deceit. They were warm and lustrous like fresh-fallen chestnuts. Heartened by the inspection, he pushed the mirror back in the drawer.

Had Suki had many lovers? It pained him to think of other men holding her in their arms, men instructed in mysteries quite unknown to him. How little he knew about these things. He trembled to think that his skills had never evolved beyond awkward fumblings behind the sofa at teenage parties, groping at some graceless form sprawled among the empty wine bottles. How gauche, how clumsy she would find him. And what else had he to offer her? It was not as if he could take her shopping, buy her clothes, or dine out at expensive restaurants. She would tire of his company within a week, a day, an hour. *The mortification of it!*

He took a deep breath, forcing himself to calm down. What had he to lose? The chance would never come again. A golden oriole had alighted on his window sill. Rebuff it, close his shutters and it would fly away, never to be seen again. The rest of his days would be spent dreaming of what might have been.

He walked back to his desk, his head down, eyes tight shut. He would leave it to the fates, let them decide. If he could put his hand on his pen among the jumble of papers before he got to a count of ten, he would accept her challenge, match her step for step, lead where it may. He started counting ... one ... two ... three... By the time he reached eight, his fingers closed around it.

Carefully, trying to keep his hand steady, he extended his footprints from their safe anchorage outside the reception room, took them down the passage ... paused for a moment by the door to the kitchen ... on past the dining room ... on the tip of his toes to the door of the bedroom ... then ... inside! The die was cast! He stood up, threw his coat over a chair and flapped his arms in an effort to cool himself. His shirt was sticking to him, perspiration was running down his sides. His whole body was trembling as if in a fever.

2

That night he tossed and turned and it was the early hours of the morning before eventually he slept. When he awoke, it was after nine. He hurled back his bedclothes and tore into the bathroom, jammed a toothbrush between his teeth and shaved around it. He had forgotten to set his alarm clock. If his father had shouted for him, he hadn't heard. Despite missing his breakfast and a great scramble to get to the underground station, he was almost an hour late at the office.

Mr Sprague came out of his room holding a mug of coffee. He looked at his watch and raised his heavy black eyebrows in mock astonishment.

'I'm sorry I'm late, Mr Sprague.'

'Work is all about discipline, Stanford. Self-discipline. I cannot chase you all the time. Time-keeping has got to become second nature.'

'Yes, Mr Sprague.'

Mr Sprague removed his glasses and polished the lens with the end of his tie. His eyes glittered like shiny black buttons. He seemed almost amiable. 'Now about Admirals Court–'

'*Has she called?* I mean, has Miss Renouf...'

'Ah, I thought that would ring the bell! Yes, she came in first thing this morning. You were probably still in bed.' Sprague opened his mouth wide to take the sting out of his gibe, showing all the fillings in his teeth. 'She wants to view the apartment at three o'clock tomorrow afternoon. You are to meet her there. Take the small Volvo.'

'Did she ask for another brochure?' He tried to keep his voice casual.

'She asked for your copy. She said that you had made some notes for her inside.' Mr Sprague nodded importantly. 'I like that, Stanford. People appreciate a little extra attention. Mark my words, young man, it always pays.' He turned to go back to his office. 'But this is just the beginning. There's a long way to go before you put this deal to bed. What matters is how you handle yourself tomorrow.'

For once Julian could not disagree.

***

He would never know how he got through the rest of the day. The pigeon strutted its stuff on the railing, up and down, up and down. Mr Sprague's feet padded on the invisible organ pedals, up and down, up and down. But he had no eyes for them. His journal stayed unopened in the drawer. His mind was far away, high up on the ninth floor in that portentous bedroom with its air of anticipation; the empty arena waiting for the gladiators to enter.

Eventually half-past five came and he left the office for the underground station. His nerves were all over the place and he had to visit a public convenience. The condition of his underclothes dismayed him. The elastic waistband was disintegrating, shedding horrible rubber crumbs. Closer examination of the garment revealed perforations unplanned by the manufacturer. He emerged once more and ran down the street, arriving at the menswear shop as it was about to close its doors. Breathlessly he explained what he wanted.

'Boxer shorts? Certainly, Sir.' The assistant produced a tape measure.

'It's alright,' Julian assured him hurriedly, 'I know my measurements.' Visits to school outfitters had given him a horror of the intimacies of the changing cubicle, the intrusive pins and proddings.

'Very good, Sir.' The assistant pulled open a drawer. 'Which style would you prefer – Oxford or Cambridge?'

Stanford stared at him, feeling his cheeks growing hot. He cursed himself for this reckless initiative. What did the man mean? His father had joked about the unique relationship between a man and his tailor, the coded language employed to convey habits of dress too personal to be transmitted openly.

'Oxford or Cambridge, Sir?' the assistant repeated patiently. 'Dark blue or light blue?'

'Oh, I see,' Stanford blurted out, feeling very foolish. He chose the light blue.

'How many pairs, Sir?' A hint of disdain in the bland expression, in the neck like a stick of celery sprouting from the stiff collar.

'Just the one ... to start with.'

'Very well, Sir. Let us know how you get on with it.'

Was the man being insolent? Stanford shot a venomous sidelong glance at him but he had turned away and was busy folding the garment into a carrier bag.

***

When he got back home he asked his mother to press his suit. She felt his forehead. 'You are rather flushed, dear. Are you sure you are not running a temperature? How about a little white briony in a glass of milk last thing?'

'No, Mother, I'm fine.' He escaped from her and ran down to his bedroom. There he laid out a clean shirt for the morning, a departure from his usual practice of turning the cuffs inside out and making it last another day. Then he hared upstairs to his father's room to ask if he could borrow a silk tie.

His father greeted him with gruff geniality, 'Got an important meeting tomorrow, old chap?'

'Yes, Father.'

'That's the stuff.' He left his son rooting around in the wardrobe and went down to the sitting room. As he poured himself a glass of dry sherry, he said to his wife, 'Julian seems to be going great guns with the new job. I have a feeling the boy is going to shape up after all.'

***

The next morning, Julian rose early and shaved with meticulous care. He dried his face and poured a little pool of aftershave into the hollow of his hand, patting it on liberally and making his cheeks tingle. After dressing, he gave himself breakfast and was waiting outside when Mr Sprague arrived to open the office.

'All fired up, Stanford? This is a big day for you.'

'I hope so, Mr Sprague.'

'I'm sure you'll do us proud.' His good humour appeared to have survived the night in his small terraced house in Acton, or North Ealing, as he told his clients. But then he sniffed. 'What's that stuff you are wearing? It smells like a sheep dip.'

Julian put a finger to his cheek. 'Only some aftershave.'

The manager pushed the key into the lock. 'You don't want to overdo things, Stanford.'

Julian's mood that morning was like the April day, sunshine and cloud. Sometimes the hands of his watch moved so slowly he was sure they must be pulling weights behind them and then suddenly they would pick up speed and race round like an electric hare at a greyhound meeting and throw him into a panic.

At midday he went across the road to the sandwich bar. There was a queue but he was so distracted that when he came to the head he hadn't decided what to order and had to go to the back again. He bought an egg roll with salad and perched on a bar stool by the window. After a single bite he put it down. Supposing it gave him an upset stomach. Egg could hardly be trusted these days and mayonnaise was no better. Leaving it on the plate, he ran his tongue around his teeth. He should have bought a toothbrush. Suki might want to kiss him. He scrubbed at his teeth with his fingers and washed out his mouth with a swig of Coca-Cola.

When Mr Sprague returned from lunch he stopped at his desk to wish him luck. 'Don't lose the keys,' he warned, 'we have only got the two sets.'

'I won't,' Julian promised.

'You did on your first day,' Liz murmured as Mr Sprague slid his newspaper from under his coat and disappeared to perform his ablutions.

'I didn't lose them,' Julian protested. 'I took the wrong ones.'

'And had to come all the way back here while the poor man hung about on the doorstep like a vagrant.' She threw a set of car keys to him. 'I ran the Volvo through the car wash so it's looking good. Try to bring it back in one piece.'

He drove slowly, following the river for a mile and a half. Outside Admirals Court there was a Rolls Royce and a Ferrari parked in front of the pillared entrance. He changed into low gear to negotiate the tight bends on the descent to the underground garage. He hadn't driven the car before and it would do nothing for his precarious reputation to return it with a crumpled wing.

Emerging from the lift at the ground floor, he was met with a salute from the porter behind the desk. 'Mr Stanford, isn't it? From Fulford Fallow? Just sign the register please, Sir. We know you of course, but we have got to stick by the rules.'

Julian signed the book. 'Have you seen–'

'The young lady, Sir? She arrived a little early and I took the liberty of showing her the solarium.'

'Are the new murals finished?'

'Yes, Sir. They had their final coat of varnish yesterday.'

'I will take a quick look.'

The porter leaned forward and rested his arms on the counter. He lowered his voice to a conspiratorial whisper. 'You will probably see Mr Skordias and his wife by the pool. They swim every afternoon and then have tea. Mrs Skordias is a very beautiful woman.' He rolled his eyes to the ceiling and described a voluptuous arabesque with his hands. 'And the dresses! The jewellery! You should see her when she goes out in the evening.' A thought occurred to him for his eyes narrowed and his voice sank to a whisper. 'If they should ever want to sell the penthouse, I will tell you first and...' his fingers tapped on his breast pocket.

Mystified, Julian stared at him for a moment but then made the connection. 'Yes ... yes ... of course ... I'm sure my firm would ... look after you.' Stanford the wheeler-dealer. Mr Sprague would be proud of him.

The porter smiled broadly and the anxious fingers returned to their place on the top of the desk.

Julian walked across the hall and pushed open a door. It was like stepping off an aeroplane into brilliant, sub-tropical sunshine. In the raised gallery that ran the length of the solarium, powerful lighting under a large glass dome created the impression of a hot white sky. Below him was a magnificent swimming pool surrounded by elegant tables and chairs shaded by colourful umbrellas. There were palm trees and behind them a *trompe d'oeil*, a panorama of hills dotted with elegant villas running down to the sparkling waters of the Mediterranean.

Two children were laughing and splashing in the blue water. An attractive young woman in her late thirties, with jet-black hair and skin like dark wheat, was emerging from the pool. She pressed her hands down the sides of her white one-piece bathing suit as if to emphasise the admirable lines of her figure. A handsome grey-haired man in a white linen suit raised himself from his chair and handed her a towelled robe. He had never seen Victor Skordias but the walnut complexion and strongly marked features left him in no doubt that it was the Greek shipping tycoon and his beautiful wife Marianna.

As he returned to the hall, Suki appeared. 'I have been looking at the river. You promised to make it blue for me. Remember?' She pouted like a sulky child. 'I don't think you are trying very hard. It turns a dreary shade of grey when the sun goes in.'

As the lift doors closed behind them, she kissed him lightly on the lips. 'Don't look so desolate,' she chided. As he tried to put his arms around her she ducked out of reach. 'How do you like my outfit?'

He stood staring at her, running his tongue over his lips, still tasting that glossy pink kiss.

'At least say you like the hat.' She tipped the straw hat with its wide blue ribbon at a rakish angle.

'It's amazing.'

'And the rest?' She performed a slow pirouette like a mechanical doll. Her jacket and skirt were white and very close-fitting, the collar and pockets trimmed in navy blue. From her shoulder a shiny white leather bag hung by long straps. She walked his fingers down the sides of her jacket, into the cinch at the waist and then over the smooth curve of the hips. 'Clothes like these make a woman feel like a woman, Mr Standfast. You don't think they are immodest?' She took his hand and laid it in the deep V of her neckline.

He snatched back his hand as if he had rested it on top of a hot stove.

Suki chortled, 'You are so amusing, Mr Standfast.' The doors opened and she stepped out onto the thick-pile carpet of the lobby. He fumbled in the pocket of his suit for the keys and would have walked ahead of her to the front door of the apartment but she put out a hand to stay him. 'Let's do everything together from now on, Mr Standfast, just as we planned.'

'Very well,' said Julian stiffly. He tucked a hand under his arm, nursing it as if it had been scorched.

'Very well,' she mimicked. She made a face at him. 'Come on, Mr Standfast, loosen up a little. Let's have some fun!'

'Fun!' he echoed bitterly. 'It's no fun being made a fool of.' Savagely he drove the key into the lock.

Turning his face to her, Suki kissed him very quickly on the tip of his nose. 'Now I have made Mr Standfast angry. I'm sorry.' She blew on his cheeks to cool them. 'How red you are! *A furious Mr Standfast!'*

He pushed open the door. 'Whatever we do, we must keep everything immaculately tidy,' he said severely.

Suki put her hands on his arms and turned him once more to face her. She was frowning. 'Whatever we do? What can you be thinking of?'

He hung his head. 'I really don't know,' he said miserably.

Suki raised her chin. 'If you don't know, I am sure I don't.' She closed the door behind them. She giggled, 'You go first. You know – just the way we rehearsed it.'

He set off across the hall. He could sense her eyes following him. He must look ridiculous. What should he do with his arms, swing them or keep them tight against his sides? And what was the layout of the apartment? It had gone clean out of his head. Liz had rushed him around it that first week. He wished that he had paid more attention. And where was the brochure? He must have left it in the car. At least it would have been something to hold.

'You must tell me what to look at,' she cried after him. 'Isn't that what estate agents are supposed to do?'

Julian waved vaguely to left and right, 'This is the hall.' What more was there to say?

He would have gone into the reception room but she called again, 'Stop there, silly. Wait for me. Can't you remember anything?' She skimmed her hat at him and he had to duck as it sailed over his head and down the passage.

He would have run after it but she came skipping up to him and, throwing her arms about him, waltzed him into the room. 'This is the reception room, Mr Standfast,' she reminded him, 'this is where I shall receive.' She steered him expertly around a coffee table and between the twin sofas. 'You are my first guest, Mr Standfast. I hope you feel honoured.'

'You do like it, Suki?' he asked anxiously. 'It would be such a help if –'

'Like it? *I adore it!* I can't live without it,' she exclaimed breathlessly as they danced past the huge picture window. '*Look, Mr Standfast!* Bridges ... and barges ... and houseboats ... and seagulls ... and, what is more, the river is blue! What a love you are – you have kept your promise!' She spun to a stop and raising his hands to her lips, ran rapid kisses along his fingers. 'Meet me outside the dining room,' she whispered, 'I need something from the kitchen.' She rounded her eyes at him and tapped her shoulder bag. Whistling a lively hornpipe, she capered through the door.

When she returned she was carrying two glasses in her hand. 'Let's have a drink, Mr Standfast!' she cried. 'We have so much to celebrate.' She stuffed the glasses into the pockets of his jacket and ran down the zipper of her bag. 'Look what I brought with me!' Taking his hand, she curled his fingers around the neck of a bottle. 'It's a Pol Roger. Isn't that just the wickedest name for champagne? If I'm the Pol ...'she pressed her pretty little teeth into her under lip, 'what does that make you?'

Stanford blushed and removed his hand quickly. 'You ... you haven't seen the ... the dining room,' he stuttered. 'The colours–'

'Show me the colours, if you insist.' Putting her arm around his waist, she peeped in through the door. 'Green and red – good for the gastric juices. How are your juices, Mr Standfast?'

'A bit subdued,' he confessed, remembering his lunchtime sandwich.

'That's too bad – just wait until you've had a glass of bubbly. You will feel like a sparkler at a birthday party.' She kicked off her shoes and ran a stockinged foot gently up the inside of his calf. 'I have had an idea, Mr Standfast.'

'Another idea?' His eyes narrowed anxiously.

'Yes, another idea.' She swayed up against him and breathed into his ear. 'Let's pretend we are courting and it's late and we have gone back to my lodgings and there's a dreadful old harridan of a landlady who will turn us onto the street if she catches us.' She took his arm, 'So, not a sound, Mr Standfast!' Like a pair of stage villains, they tiptoed up the passage to the door of the bedroom.

'Look at that bed!' Suki shrieked. 'I have always wanted a brass bed.' She dropped her bag, threw off her jacket and, sprinting across the room, took a running dive across the satin counterpane. Seizing the brass rail,

she pulled herself up to the foot of the bed. 'Let's play lions and tigers, Mr Standfast.' She tossed her golden mane from side to side and made low growling sounds at him from between the bars.

Julian picked Suki's jacket off the floor and placed it over the arm of a chair. 'We mustn't make so much noise. Supposing–'

'I can't help myself. I feel wild and tempestuous. You will have to tame me. Do you think you could tame me, Mr Standfast?'

'I'm not sure...' he said doubtfully.

Suki rolled over onto her back and stretched out her arms to him. 'Pour me a drink, lover,' she entreated. She rolled her eyes upwards and caught sight of the picture above the bed, '*Look at that picture, Mr Standfast!*' With a squeal of pleasure she jumped to her feet, bouncing up and down on the bed. 'All fauns and frolics! *Isn't it just shameless?*'

As he tried to fill her glass, Suki shaped her lips for a kiss. His lips parted, seeking hers. Suki leaned down, looked deep into his eyes and blew a cloud of froth at him. She collapsed on the bed gurgling with laughter. 'If you could see yourself, you poor darling. You have got bubbles on the end of your nose.' Throwing back the counterpane, she plumped up the pillows, stretched out and, with a little sigh, closed her eyes.

Stanford took the dripping glass from her fingers before it tumbled to the floor and placed it on the table. His blood was running like a tide race. He threw off his jacket and tie, half expecting to see steam rising from his shirt. Suki opened her eyes and raised herself on her elbow but he pressed her shoulders down onto the bed.

'I want you, Suki.' In his ears, his voice sounded as thick as treacle.

She swung up her legs and lifted him off her as neatly as a mechanic raising a car on a hydraulic ramp. She rolled to the other side of the bed and sat up. 'You go too quickly, my sweet.' She pushed her hair back off her forehead. 'Calm down or you will spoil everything.'

He grabbed his glass and drained it at a single gulp. His fingers fumbled at the buttons of his shirt. For the life of him he could not stop trembling. His nerves were vibrating like harp strings. 'I'm sorry, Suki,' he muttered, 'my feelings ran away with me.'

'Run after them and catch them, Mr Standfast. Tell them to behave. Feelings are like small children. They demand treats all the time. Tell them to be patient.'

'How can I be patient, Suki, when I feel ... like ... like this?'

'Like what, Mr Standfast?' she teased, trailing her fingers through his hair.

He groaned. 'You know how I feel. Why torture me?'

Suki stood up. She took his hands and, pressing them to her lips, looked into his eyes. 'You should see your face, Mr Standfast. It's all lined and twisted as if you had a migraine.'

'Oh! Suki! Please–'

'Try to be good for a little longer. When I have had my bath–'

'A bath! You're not–'

'Certainly I must bathe. You should too.'

'I had a bath this morning.'

'Well, I didn't. Turn on the taps for me, there's a pet.'

He went into the bathroom. All mirrors and marble. Bending down, he lifted a corner of a towel and brushed it against his cheek, searching for the fragrance, the softness that her body would lend it. He kissed it and pressed it gently through the ring above the bath. He let the water run slowly, allowing it to trickle through his fingers ... this water that would hold her ... encompass her...

As he came back into the bedroom, Suki was tucking in the sheet at the foot of the bed. She straightened quickly. 'You look as red as a turkey cock, Mr Standfast. Are you terribly excited?'

'It's all this waiting, Suki.'

'I won't be long. I swear it.' She placed his hand against her heart for a long moment and then returned it to him. 'Think about me while you wait or, better still, play the undressing game.'

'What's the–'

'Don't talk. *Watch!*' She raised the hem of her skirt and reaching underneath, rolled her stockings slowly down her long, silky smooth legs. Julian felt his mouth drying, his heartbeat quicken.

'Every time you bare a new part of your body,' she explained, 'you must promise it a treat. Start with each of your toes and work upwards.' She ran down a zipper and, with a deft wiggle of her behind, shuffled her skirt down to her ankles. Hooking the skirt with her toes, she hoisted it neatly onto a chair and skipped off towards the bathroom.

He glowered at her retreating figure. 'What did you promise your ... I mean ... the part you bared...?'

Suki plucked a bath towel from the rail and threw it to him. '*Unimaginable delight*, Mr Standfast. That's what I promised myself. I have great expectations of you. You must live up to them.'

She had left the door ajar. He listened acutely. Above the sound of the running water, she was singing to herself. And then came the clink of buttons on the marble floor. Her blouse. She had removed her blouse. Her hands would be reaching behind her for the hooks of her brassiere. Unfastening ... freeing her breasts ... now she was padding over to the bath ... bending over the edge to test the temperature of the water ... her body curved like a drawn bow ... then dipping her finger into the warmth, stirring it into excited ripples ... straightening again ... sliding her fingers under the waistband of her...

'Are your shoes and socks off yet, Mr Standfast?'

He reached down to tug off a shoe. 'Almost...'

'Promise each of your toes a little treat,' Suki reminded him. 'The treats get more thrilling as you go higher.'

Barefoot, he walked over to the window and stared out through the balcony railings to the river. The cars crawling across the bridges looked no larger than toys, the office blocks like models on a town planner's board. What would they say, the people down there, inching along in the traffic or languishing in their cell-like offices, tapping away at their dreary keyboards. What would they say if they could see him now, if they could raise their heads from their Lilliputian existence to–

'Are you undressed yet, Mr Standfast? Wonderfully, gloriously naked?'

'Not quite, Suki.' He undid the buttons on his shirt and let his belt out a hole. Suddenly he needed a drink.

He refilled his glass, drained it at a single gulp and replenished it once more.

He could hear her splashing out of the bath ... patting herself dry. He let out his belt another hole and plucked at the top of his trunks. He wished now that he had chosen the Oxford blue. How could he have chosen that washed-out colour? It was the colour of funk. Blue funk. And his skin – how pale it was. His arms – how thin they looked. It was his mother's fault. She had passed on her skinniness to him.

Wonderfully, gloriously naked! What a travesty of manliness Suki would think him. The shame! The humiliation! It was not to be borne! His eyes flashed to the door. If he fled, ran now – there was time – still just time enough to grab his clothes – make a dash for it. He groaned out aloud.

'I won't be long now, lover.'

Where were his socks? He ran across the carpet. The room looked like the aftermath of a jumble sale. Frantically he cast around for his shoes. And his jacket ... his tie...

'I wonder what Mr Sprague would say if he could see us now.'

Julian stopped dead. *Mr Sprague!* For a moment he had forgotten the man. He must get back ... but if he ran now... No! Suki wasn't the sort of woman that men would leave. At least not like this. She would go crazy! She would ring Sprague! Scream down the telephone! In her fury she might say anything. That he had assaulted her! Lured her to this apartment and tried to rape her! He would get back to the office and find the police waiting for him. *Oh, God! What was he to do!*

'Coming, lover...'

It was too late. In a panic he dumped the collection of oddments at his feet, threw off his remaining clothes, all save the disparaged shorts, wrapped the bath towel tight about him, scrambled into bed and pulled the covers to his chin.

Suki came out of the bathroom like a swan alighting on water, her white bathrobe spreading like wings as, with a huge leap, she landed at his side. With a yelp of glee she tore back the bedclothes and threw them on the floor. His hands clutched at the towel, 'No! Suki! *Don't!*' But with wonderful adroitness she reached under it and tugged his shorts down to his ankles and over his wildly threshing feet.

'*You lying hound!* You said that you were gloriously naked!' She rolled the shorts into a tight ball and hurled them across the room where they came to rest on the dressing table.

'Please, Suki–'

She covered his face with kisses, 'You are a cheat, Mr Standfast. That is what you are. And cheats have to be punished.' She spread herself over him and placing her forehead against his, fluttered his eyelids with her long lashes. 'You have guilty eyes, Mr Standfast.'

'Suki, no–'

'Yes, you have. I believe you almost ran out on me.'

'No, Suki. I promise–'

'Do you know what I wrote on the bathroom mirror? I wrote, "I love Mr Standfast" in that beautiful pink soap smelling of strawberries. I have a good mind to scrub it all off and write "Mr Standfast is a rat."'

'It's not true, Suki!'

'*Prove it!*' She ran the tip of her tongue around the lobe of his ear and then in a moist trail down his neck to his shoulder. 'Does this delight you, Mr Standfast?'

'It's won … d …der … f … ful!'

'It's going to get better.' Gently she ran kisses along his fingers, nuzzling for the damp palm of his hand until he released his hold on the towel. Slipping to his side, she laid him bare to the waist.

'No, Suki! *No!*' Her mouth came down on his, stifling all protest. He felt his lips swelling, the walls of his nostrils widening as his body cried out for air. Sensation tracked through him like a thermal vest wired up to a power station.

'As long as you live, Mr Standfast, you will never forget this afternoon.' She printed kisses up the inside of his arm, following the long blue vein from the wrist to the shoulder. 'And that's a promise.' She cradled his arm in her hands, fondling it as if it was the dearest part of him, running her cheek along its length, stretching it gently at the elbow, moving it higher, easing it away from his body like a door swinging back on well-oiled hinges.

As she stretched over him, her robe was drawn back from her shoulders. The scent of her was borne to him like a break in the weather ... the air closer ... heavier ... charged with her. The fingers of his right hand, seeking extra purchase, closed on the head rail ... he raised his head ... his lips seeking hers ... with his left hand he swept the towel free of his body. There was a sharp 'click!' as the steel jaws closed around his wrist.

Julian squawked in sudden terror, '*What's this*!' He gave a violent tug at the chain which secured him to the rail and cried out in pain as the metal sawed at his skin. 'What … what have you done to me?'

Suki rolled to his side. 'It's only a game, Mr Standfast,' she soothed. 'I didn't mean to startle you.'

With his free hand, Julian clutched his burning wrist. 'You hurt me, Suki.'

'I didn't mean to, sweetheart. It's only a love game.' She shushed his moans with kisses. 'Lie still. Abandon yourself to your feelings.' Her fingers trotted over his body like a file of infantry in open, lightly defended country. They made little feints here, forays there, running swiftly over the exposed places, lingering in the sparse cover afforded. 'Promise me you won't resist,' she whispered. The fingers jogged down his left leg.

'I promise,' he mumbled. Recovering rapidly from his shock, he was beginning to enjoy himself. Why not leave everything to Suki? For one as untutored as he, there were great attractions.

'Do you surrender to me, darling Mr Standfast? Unconditionally?'

'I do.' In his ears it sounded like a marriage vow. He stretched luxuriously. When she gently secured his ankle to the rail at the bottom of the bed and ran a line of kisses along the top of his toes, he merely smiled and closed his eyes.

'Now you are my prisoner. You must do everything I say.' She knelt between his knees. 'Do you think you could do it three times, Mr Standfast, if I–'

'*Of course not!*' Aghast, Stanford tried to sit up but his bonds held him fast. 'It's im … im … possible!'

'How do you know,' she coaxed, 'unless you try?'
Her eyes widened and her fingers stole into the pocket
of her robe.

'What have you got there?' His voice rose in fear.
'I'm not taking any drugs. My heart couldn't stand it.
I've heard of people like–'

'People like me! There's no one like me! Not in the
whole wide world! Admit it!'

'I admit it.'

She withdrew her hand. 'And they aren't drugs.'
Her tongue flicked around the inside of his lips. 'They
are medals, Mr Standfast. A bronze, a silver ... look!'
Gently, she positioned the objects in the hollows of his
eyes like a jeweller's glass.

'They are napkin rings.'

'To me they are medals. Olympic medals. When
you have won them you will be entitled to wear them.'

'Where?'

'Where do you think?'

Stanford blinked rapidly as his brain struggled to
reach any other interpretation but the obvious one. As
his lips opened in stupefaction, Suki furled her tongue
and drove it between them like a scoop into a bowl of
cherries. As his body arched upwards, reaching for her,
she whisked the towel from under him as neatly as a
conjuror and threw it across the room. With a
mischievous twitch of her nostrils, she poised the rings
between finger and thumb.

Horrified, he followed the direction of her eyes.
'Not there, Suki!' He jerked his body to one side crying
out as his bonds bit into his flesh, *'No!'*

'Why not?' She twirled the rings on her finger.
'Bronze – tortoiseshell was all I could find. And silver.

As for the gold...' She picked up the foil from the champagne bottle.

'*You're not going to use that!*'

'Of course I am.' It was the work of a few moments to fashion the third ring. 'Now, Mr Standfast. Let's try them on for size.'

His free hand flew to cover himself. 'Don't do it, Suki,' he pleaded, 'it's not fair.'

'Come on, lover. Be a sport.'

'Never.' His head was shaking like a coconut in a gale, 'Never! *Never!*'

'Well, if you feel like that...' she built a small pagoda of the rings on his navel, slipped off the bed and trotted across the room.

'*Suki!* Where are you going?'

She did not answer. Shrugging off her robe, she pulled the door to and disappeared into the passage.

'*Suki!*' he yelled. '*Come back!*' He heaved at his fetters and then fell limply back once more. Don't panic, you fool, he told himself. There's nothing to get so stewed up about. Suki had left her shoulder bag in the passage. She had probably gone to do things about herself. Woman's business. How naive she must think him. How foolish he was to have shouted. Any moment now she would be back. His throat was dry. If he could reach the bottle ... his eyes fell on his watch. The time! He couldn't see the face. What was the time? He brought his free arm across his body ... but no ... he couldn't get his fingers near the table.

Making his hand as small as possible, he tried to force it through the ring which held it. It was no use. He was powerless. Things couldn't go on like this. It must be getting late. Mr Sprague would expect him back. With the deal done.

Putting all the authority into his voice that he could muster, he raised his voice once more. He spoke slowly and severely. '*Suki!* Miss Renouf!' Was she Miss or Mrs – or even Ms? Why hadn't he been given more information about this woman? It was intolerable. He would speak to Mr Sprague about it. Or to Mr Fallow if he had to.

'*Suki!* There are one or two things we need to get straightened out. *At once!* Admirals Court is the best property that we have on our books. There is a lot of interest in it. The views from the ninth floor...' his voice tailed off. She knew about the views. Get to the point. Behave like Liz Makin. Punchy. Assertive. 'It is obvious that you like it here, Suki. And you say the rent is not a problem.' What was the rent? Had he been told? He couldn't remember discussing it with Suki. Wasn't that one of the first questions people asked? 'So let's get down to business, Suki. Time marches on...' he concluded miserably.

This was getting him nowhere. There was a limit to how far one could pursue unilateral negotiations. '*Suki!*' he bellowed, 'Come back! *Immediately!*' Where was she? When he considered all the trouble he had been put to. '*Suki!*'

He shivered. There was a chill in the air. If he could reach the edge of the sheet where it tucked in, pull it out and over him. But no, it was impossible. And it was torture trying. He lay back with a groan.

He started at a different sound. Above the hum of the world beyond the window, the clunk of metal on metal. A grapnel hooking onto a rail. It would sound just like that. A short length of rope swung past the window. A sharp intake of breath. She would be stretching up, grasping the rope, pulling her light, lithe body up to the balcony above. Then a thin scratching like chalk on a blackboard – or a diamond cutting into a glass pane. Then, a faint rustling sound. He knew that noise. Venetian blinds disturbed by a window being opened.

Then footsteps, the sound muffled by a thick carpet. With his eyes he tracked the steps across the ceiling until they stopped immediately over the dressing table. A patter like hailstones. The Skordias jewellery. Priceless gemstones scattered for inspection, selection, retention.

Footsteps again, padding over to the door, now receding. Then silence. Then the murmur of the lift ascending, passing his floor, rising to the penthouse flat above him. He strained his ears for the gentle sigh of doors opening and closing. The lift descending once more. Suki leaving. Going down, down, down to the netherworld from which she had come. Leaving with everything she came for. Leaving without him. Leaving him here. Alone.

How cold it was. As cold as a tomb. With his free hand he tried to chafe his skin, rub some warmth into his limbs. His medals, unearned, unclaimed, rolled off his body to the floor. He wished that it was all over. That he was dead, extinct, like a starfish beached by the tide, inert when the gulls, wheeling and screaming, swooped down with their ravening beaks.

With the passing of time, faint stirrings of hope returned to him. Victor Skordias was an important visiting businessman entitled to the protection of the host country. His trust had been betrayed, his possessions pillaged. The government would do everything to prevent the news getting out. There would be a top-level cover-up. The Secretary of State for the Environment would come around in person in the dead of night and remove the number from the door. The apartment would be walled up and all records of the ninth floor of Admirals Court expunged from public records. He would simply be left there. Mr Sprague would be bribed with a knighthood to keep quiet. It would be as if he had never existed, as if what had taken place here had never–

The hum of the lift again. Doors opening. Voices. A man and a woman. The woman's voice high, nasal, with a captious 'nothing but the best will do' edge to it. 'It's a long way up. I certainly hope it's worth it.'

The man ingratiating, 'The views are quite remarkable, I assure you, Madam.' *Mr Sprague!*

'Well, we shall soon see.' The key turning in the latch. The voices more distinct.

Gritting his teeth against the pain, Stanford heaved at his chains. But it was futile. Not an inch did they give. *'O God!'* he babbled, *'don't let them come in ... do something ... something appalling ... an earthquake ... a volcanic eruption ... a tidal wave! You know You can do it if You try!'*

The voices approaching up the passage. 'One or two small things out of place...' A hint of unease in Mr Sprague's portentous delivery. 'Perhaps we should start at the master bedroom ... I know you will be impressed with that.'

'Has the daily woman been here? You *do* have a daily woman who comes in?'

'Not since ... not since this morning, Madam. One of our negotiators had a viewing here this afternoon. Sometimes one or two little things get disarranged.' The voices very near now.

No closer, Stanford prayed ... please no closer ... don't let them open the door ... let me off this ... this last time ... I'll never ask for anything else ... I'll do anything ... I'll grow up ... wear a suit all the time like father ... sit at a desk all day ... become old and angry ... have tufts in my ears...

The voices as loud as the trumpets on the Day of Judgement. Stanford's eyes bulged in his head, the muscles in his face went solid like quick-drying cement, his free leg writhed despairingly ... with his hand he tried to cover himself.

'The negotiator? He's a young chap called Julian Stanford. Joined us a week or two ago.' The voices at the door now. 'A most promising lad,' the handle turning, 'and really keen to show us what he's made of...'

In Brief

Charles Owen writes the Army obituaries for the Daily Telegraph. He has been variously a stockbroker, a merchant banker, a cavalry officer, a Ministry of Defence contractor and an engineering export salesman. *Cry Cassandra*! and *Fiamma* were published recently. Four collections of short stories – *A Crack in the Glass, The Mark of the Beast, Man Overboard* and *Escapade* – are now being published simultaneously.

Meet the Author, Charles Owen

I was born in 1935. When the Second World War broke out a few years later, I was shipped off from a Devonshire hill farm to Australia. My father, who was wounded in the First World War, was then in MI5. He believed that the Germans might invade and probably wanted my mother, sister and myself out of the way.

In 1942, we were returning to England when we were torpedoed by a German submarine in the North Atlantic. The ship was sent to the bottom but after taking to the waves in a lifeboat we were all rescued by the US Navy.

Aged 12, I went to Eton. Top hats were being phased out. They were routinely maltreated until the boys wearing them looked like something out of the music hall. But if the school was slowly changing, the house where I boarded lacked all mod cons and was later pulled down.

In 1956, in my first term at Cambridge and despite the objections of the Foreign Office, I set off to Budapest in the hope of helping the Hungarians in their revolution against the Soviets. My involvement made little difference to the outcome of that tragic affair but the experience provided the inspiration for my forthcoming book, *The Dido Decrypt*.

I did my National Service with a cavalry regiment in Germany. Our job was to discourage the Red Army from crossing the Rhine. As a tank commander, it was wise to keep well in with your driver. If he was cross with you, he would give you a bumpy ride which would loosen every tooth in your head.

A spell in stock-broking and merchant banking persuaded me that I was better at making things than making money and there followed many productive years as the export director of an engineering company. We were contractors to the Ministry of Defence and there was a lot of travelling to the Middle East. The work was absorbing, exacting and, sometimes, frightening.

In 2000, for the Daily Telegraph, I began writing up the stories of the surviving men and women who had been awarded the Victoria Cross or the George Cross. That led to writing the obituaries of those who had had adventurous and distinguished careers in the British Army. To date, several hundred of these can be read on the internet.

In the course of reading private papers and unpublished memoirs that have passed through my hands, I became fascinated by the exciting and often perilous careers of servicemen and women who were involved in Intelligence operations; spies and counter-spies, secret agents and members of the Special Operations Executive who were parachuted into enemy-occupied countries to train and arm the Resistance. *The Voce Vendetta*, relating the fictional exploits of Captain Rohan Voce, will be published in 2016 and will, I hope, bring an account of some of these clandestine operations to a wider readership.

Acknowledgements

My heartfelt thanks go to Georgie, my daughter, who helped to unravel the seemingly impenetrable mysteries of the word processor, also to my son, Jamie, whose guidance has proved invaluable in my wanderings through the trackless wastes of journalism; and to Pierre, my brother-in-law, whose expertise, unstintingly shared, kept my spirits up and my blood pressure down when the hardware and software sulked or threatened to mutiny. I have nothing but praise for the unwinking editorial eyes of the proof-readers. Rosie, heroically volunteered to give the manuscript a final vetting. Any errors that remain are my responsibility.